Sharing Light

Sharing Light

Stories of Christmas

Tim Morrison

authorHOUSE®

AuthorHouse™
1663 Liberty Drive
Bloomington, IN 47403
www.authorhouse.com
Phone: 1-800-839-8640

First published by AuthorHouse 10/21/2011

ISBN: 978-1-4670-6273-2 (sc)
ISBN: 978-1-4670-6272-5 (hc)
ISBN: 978-1-4670-6271-8 (ebk)

Library of Congress Control Number: 2011918366

Printed in the United States of America

This book is printed on acid-free paper.

With love to Eva and Terri

Contents

Introduction

As the winter blizzards of 1977 buried Benedictine College, students who were excited to journey home stayed behind awaiting safer driving conditions, celebrating the conclusion of final exams, and sharing time with friends. At the urging of friends, I reluctantly presented a story I'd written as a simple expression of thanksgiving to my parents. Students, many whom I had never met, gathered from our residence halls and nestled with blankets and pillows like little children to listen. As I read, I shared my gratitude and love through a vision while the elements of cold and darkness fell away to warmth and light.

Many asked if I'd celebrate with them again next Christmas. I thought, "I couldn't repeat the same story" so I wrote another. But why for over thirty years, craft stories and 'why' especially at Christmas?

The mysteries of Christmas are woven into our experience. Collectively, I try to expose their essence in the lives of my characters. Each story has a living Spirit with elements of truth, beauty, love . . . all illuminating our lives in a brilliant way.

Our gifts are our 'selves,' our presence. Being 'present' to share, to break bread together, to welcome each other is, by far, greater than the anticipation of an event.

Christmas has always been a paradox of hope and anxiety. The two often generate turbulence within our lives. Even Mary 'pondered' the birth of her son and the events surrounding Jesus' life. Parents experience immeasurable joys with the birth of a child, a gift beyond words' descriptions. As parents marvel at their infant's miraculous entry into the world, they also ponder, having more questions than answers. What just happened? How do we care for one so fragile? What challenges and responsibilities lie in the future? What changes personally must we make? How will we react knowing there may be no answers to some questions?

I imagine an obscure infant Jesus born on a quiet eve among livestock bedded in straw. I see Him feeding the hungry, healing the sick, comforting the wounded, lifting the lowly, and challenging the wise. It is when I fail to ponder Christ's suffering and dying before the very people he ministered that I find God's intervention, His participation in the world, to be like the birth of his Son, modest, unassuming, ambiguous, unconventional, nonsensical, and definitely mysterious.

Though we have amazing technologies to network with others, we are failing to communicate. From the Latin word *communicatus* meaning to share or to impart, today's networks do neither. Mass media, owned and directed by a few, sensationalize greed, anger, genocide, economic and physical abuse, and the prostitution of others . . . amplifying anxiety and fear. My faith is riddled with threads of doubt. And, yet, there are those inspired days I do trust the world lies in the Light. Unfortunately, our God, *extremely patient and committed to our free will*, will not wipe away our mess. He/She has given us generous, loving individuals living among us. We must not isolate ourselves in an insincere network of babble. Despite our brokenness, failures, and ignorance, we must step into the Light. If we ponder our lives, look closely, we will find God revealed through our experiences and relationships in wounds and healing, tragedy and celebration, death and rebirth.

I am broadcasting 'hope' as I find it. I invite others to 'tune in' to the genuine mysteries of those living each 'story.' Break free from fear and artificial self-esteem promising superficial optimism. Live in true, resilient hope.

I appeal to all in faith of a Spirit living in each of us . . . a Spirit of goodness, peace, compassion, and love. Find redemption and light within yourself and in others through living in community. Though often turbulent, Christmas is a season of anticipation, forgiveness, healing, mystery, rebirth, and relationships. With innocence and trust, each must welcome and nurture the innate 'heart of a child.'

Inspiration comes... often in the whisper of my experience. In the northern hemisphere, the season of Christmas falls during the darkest month of the year. Christmas is a time of reflection . . . to seek Light in the darkness . . . to slow down to be present . . . to give of one's self.

Today, anticipation grows from the seeds of tradition. As a science teacher amongst Bunsen burners for candles and flaming ions for ambiance, I present to my students, friends, colleagues, peers, and strangers . . . my annual Christmas story. Later, I travel west to celebrate with family and friends.

I write to proclaim the mystery and hope in the lives of others who know struggle, make mistakes, and risk stepping into the Light to scatter it forward.

I am responding to the Whisper to present through my life and those of others' ideals which have become reality. I challenge the reader to leave abstract ideals and to form relationships, to live in communion with others. Find hope breathing in the relationships of family, friends, and beyond . . . in the lives of strangers. The brevity of these stories fails to capture the magnitude of time that elapses in our lives and the lives of the characters.

I desire a hopeful future. I write to reveal hope sewn in the fabric of dissonance and goodness. I know I am not a great writer, but I present the greatness in others' lives, the uplifting Spirit, the Light which struck our spinning globe over four billion years ago and continues to fill each of us each day.

I write the stories to be presented orally, though definitely not required. I invite you to share a moment to engage your family and friends. I hope the stories invite you to the Spirit, the essence of Christmas and that you as the reader take pause with courage and humility to ponder and accept the gifts of your family, friends, and experiences!

Merry Christmas,
Tim Morrison

Footnote

I invite you to share an experience, read a story to others. In your giving, you will also give to those in need. I hope I inspire generosity in you and the community. Though this is just a small collection of my Christmas stories, the proceeds of the sales of these stories go to help those in need, many of whom have inspired me. You will find a partial list of charities these stories support listed in the Notes section of this book. It is my dream to establish a charitable foundation. Please look for my related website in the near future. Thank you.

It's a World for Love

The Christ Child's eyes blurred. The once tender, comforting touch of her lips gracing his cheek reduced to memory.

Brian's heart raced ahead of him as a crisp breeze swept through his jet-black hair. The farther he ran, the more his legs wobbled like jelly. Fearless, he halted.

Short of breath, the small ten-year-old gasped, "I'm out."

Vigilantly, the boy walked along the cleared sidewalk. Scouting the path ahead and behind, he searched for anyone suspiciously following him. He slid along the sidewalk, methodically kicking the shoveled snow crowding the edge. Scanning the sky, he studied a clouded array of inverted, gray pillows, stuffed with snow. Trees in the neighborhood bared their branches. Footprints of children and pets littered the worn white blanket covering the ground. The day before Christmas catered to last-minute bargain hunters.

Brian suffered, dreaming about how the auto accident that claimed his parents' lives must have occurred. His imagination crafted agonizing scenarios for he knew no details of the tragedy. Uprooted from his neighborly hometown, Springdale, he failed to find fertile soil at Marian's Home in Denver. Living in Marian's environment of regimented rules stifled his spirit. He spent his ninth year of life in the brick structure occupied by troubled adolescents. Every night at the posted time, he claimed his bed among three others sharing his room.

During an extended recess while most battled beneath a barrage of snowballs, Brian squeezed between two iron posts of a fence circling the playground. Taking advantage of the distracted attendants, he ran much faster and farther than any timed event he'd run against his peers.

What road led to Springdale and friends?

Cold air slapped his cheeks. His stomach growled for a hard salami sandwich. Perhaps escaping just before noon was a poor decision. Ignoring wisdom, he compromised hunger, rest, and shelter. His body lost the enthusiastic heat it acquired during his clandestine jaunt. The cold penetrated his coat. Crystals falling from above patched the white blanket below. He resigned from kicking any more snow. His clammy toes stiffened.

As he approached the corner, he heard faint crying. His glassy blue eyes scanned the tightly packed row of houses lining the neighborhood. A disturbing siren sounded to his left. Pivoting on the curb, he isolated a toddler lying in the snow. Sprinting as fast as his tired legs would carry him, he converged on the boy.

As Brian drew near, he discovered the boy had slid down a short, but steep embankment in the front yard. Unable to correct for pitch, the little tike repeatedly climbed two steps and slid back, again. Failure to conquer the slope spawned frustration.

Gently, Brian spoke as not to startle the little one. "Hey, may I help you?"

Surprised, the child ceased crying.

"Come here." Brian stepped behind him. "I'll help you."

Clutching him under the arms, Brian struggled to swing him up and over the icy rise. Upon reaching the doorbell,

Brian summoned help with the rescue. Seconds later, a young mother answered.

Glancing at the pair, she caught a glimpse of her son. "What are you doing with Fredrick?" She reached for her son's hand and led him to her side.

"He slipped down the hill." Brian pointed. "Crying, he'd try to climb up, but he couldn't."

"Well, thank you," she stuttered, "I haven't ever seen you around here. Do you live in the neighborhood?"

"I don't . . ." Silent, he almost conceded the brief success he struggled so hard to achieve. Composing his thoughts, he pointed figuratively to a distant area. "I live about three blocks from here."

Despite her toddler's tugging for freedom, she clasped his snow pants. "Again, thank you for helping Fredrick. I hope you have a merry Christmas."

"You too!" Brian turned and slid down the short slope as the youngster's mother ushered him inside.

The snowfall thickened. The frigid air wisped against his neck forcing a shiver to slither down his spine. His toes and fingertips constantly reminded him he needed warmth.

Daylight surrendered to gaudy and classy light displays alike. Business hours expired. Traffic lined the avenue. As he trudged through the slush, a black and white object attracted his attention. Shrill whimpering resounded from a snow bank. Closing the gap, Brian discovered an abandoned puppy.

The small creature struggled to break free. Digging into the snow, Brian lifted the pup. A two-inch cut hampered its right hip. Straddling the pup's legs over his forearm, Brian fingered the wound. The puppy yelped in pain. He gently nestled the dog beneath his coat, cradling it in such a way as to form a tiny cushion. In silence, he felt it shiver from the cold.

Continuing, he finally reached the major intersection. He looked both directions along the avenue. Buildings displayed magnificent arrays of color, each topped with a conical tree creating an elevated electric forest. Spectral flakes danced in the turbulence of passing cars.

The signal flashed green. The refugee skated across the slippery pavement. Upon entering a department store, warmth thawed his frozen shell. The puppy had fallen asleep. But to verify he wasn't dead, Brian squeezed his supporting hand. Wiggling to reestablish his comfortable position, the pup continued to sleep.

Brian wound through cluttered aisles to Santa's Workshop. A young girl occupied Santa's lap. Upon observation, this Santa appeared quite young. Brian knew Santa to be a fictional character. He quickly evaluated. *This Santa should have been older. What a ridiculous, unfortunate fraud,* he thought.

Santa gave a striped candy cane to the child and rose from his throne. She waved and disappeared into a sea of aisles.

Brian scampered toward Santa hollering. "Wait, Santa! Wait!"

The man in costume turned and assumed his winter throne. "Ho, ho, ho," he bellowed, "what can I do for you, young man?"

Kris Kringle directed the lad to sit on his lap. "What is your name?" The white bearded impersonator wrapped his bulky arm around his final visitor.

"Brian."

"And Brian, what do you want for Christmas?" he chuckled.

"I want to be happy for Christmas."

"Is that all . . . no toys?"

Brian hesitated. He didn't want to compromise his identity. Studying Santa's lively brown eyes and peaceful nature, the escapee considered surrendering the day's events for complete freedom. Time dissolved into the puddle at his feet. He made his decision.

"You're not Santa Claus," he scolded. You're too young. Besides, my mom and dad told me all about Santa. You've got it all wrong."

"Ho, ho, ho, I'll tell you what," Kris compromised, "if you don't tell a single soul, I'll give you **two** candy canes. And . . . I'll bet . . . Santa comes to your house, tonight."

He relinquished the ransom of two candy canes.

Brian vaulted from Santa's lap and dashed to the front door. Pulling it open, he turned and yelled back, "I'll bet not!"

A couple hours ticked away. Pausing to rest, the fugitive entered the Holy Family Church. Warmth bathed him once again. A simple Nativity scene generously lit for display filled an ornate archway in the sacristy. A few elderly meditated on the essence of that night nearly two millennia ago as they anticipated the midnight celebration. Brian strolled down the aisle and sat on the marble steps leading to the manger sheltering the crib and a statue of the Christ Child. Sheep, oxen, cattle, shepherds, parents, and angels attended the newborn.

The Child's eyes stared into his own. Words from the past penetrated his thoughts. *He is a very important child.* His mother's voice created the story of the Nativity. He felt her gentle arms wrapped around his neck and her soft, smooth cheek touch his own. In a pleasant voice, she whispered. *Mary and Joseph were very poor. Nobody had room for Mary in the inn. She was pregnant with a baby. Joseph gathered straw and made beds for them in an old manger that housed farm animals. Joseph, a fine carpenter, built a crib and filled it with straw. Soon after, Mary gave birth to a baby boy. He was a gift promised from the good Lord.*

"What's so good about that?"

That little boy offered love and offered the world peace and joy.

"He did?"

Yes, he did. It is something like when you were born. You brought your father and me much closer together in love and devotion. Presents don't make people happy. It's the joy and love you give them. We would rather have you more than anything else in the entire world.

Tears trickled across Brian's cheeks. He could not hear her voice any more. She was gone. Why? The Christ Child's eyes blurred. The once tender, comforting touch of her lips gracing his cheek reduced to memory.

The skinny runt demanded food, scratching and squirming beneath the boy's coat. Squelching his sobbing, Brian cradled his puppy. As he reached into his pocket, he unwrapped a candy cane and set it on the material before the dog's nose. Satisfied, the pup licked the sweet treat.

Drying his eyes with the sleeve of his coat, Brian rose and descended the steps quietly. The longer he lingered within, the more memories overwhelmed him, harnessing his quest for freedom.

Snow accumulated. Faint caroling drifted from behind. Rushing—around the corner, the ten-year-old nearly crashed into a large crowd. He heard their voices, but he couldn't see the source. "The First Noel" cut through the thick snow. His puppy slept.

Enveloped into the crowd, "Silent Night's" harmony flooded his thoughts. Last year, when his family attended an outdoor Christmas concert, his father lifted and propped him on his shoulders. He saw every choir member.

Before he could react to his reflection, a voice pierced the background vocals.

"Leave me alone. I want to go home." A gruff, sober child stomped away from her parents.

Separating from the crowd, she pouted and fussed while her parents enjoyed the performance. "O Holy Night" challenged her. Brian refused to tolerate it. *Why should she be unhappy?*

He approached the girl of his own age. Arms folded as a barrier, she sported a cream colored coat trimmed with a chestnut collar. He'd like to trade for her mittens, scarf, and snow boots. Sulking wrinkled her freckled face. Thin patches of blond hair peeked from beneath her stocking cap with a fluffy blue ball on the top.

He questioned. "What's wrong? It's Christmas."

With her hazel eyes aglow, she snapped, "Why don't you quit bugging me?"

"I didn't mean to bug you. I just don't understand your mood."

"What's your name anyway?" she cross-examined sternly.

"Brian."

"Okay, Brian." She cocked her hands on her hips. "What do you want?"

"Why aren't you happy?"

"Maybe because you're bugging me . . . Hey, look, I asked for a bunch of things for Christmas. I know I'm not going to get them."

"How do you know?" Unsure what to say next, he curbed his curiosity.

"Because, they told me. I never have. All my friends always get the cool stuff." She glanced away attempting to ignore him. "What do you know anyway?"

"Look around you." he offered without criticism. "See all of those people smiling and singing. See how happy they are?"

"Yea, I see. Most of them are moms and dads," she stated sarcastically.

"The moms and dads are happy 'cause God's showin' His love tonight. None of those people are happy because they're going to get lots of presents. They're happy because they love each other."

"God sent us a baby boy so He could unite us and make us happy. Look at it this way, when your mom and dad had you, you brought more love to them **and** they like you and everyone more."

Brian's puppy stirred beneath his coat.

"What's that?" She stared at his coat.

"My hand twitched. Kinda cold. I forgot my good gloves."

"That's sorta dumb."

He quickly redirected her attention to her parents. "Look at your mom and dad. Sure, they're smiling, but not very big. Walk over to them and I'll bet they'll be a lot happier. Love and happiness with your family and friends are what Christmas is all about. Your mom and dad love you more than anything in the world."

"How do you know? I don't see your parents," she challenged. "Did you make them happy?"

His eyes avoided hers to pan the gathering. "I hope so."

"Don't you know?" She questioned his credibility.

"They aren't here anymore." Silence quenched the verbal fire. Brian pushed her firmly toward her parents. "Go on. I'll bet you!"

He wandered across the street seeking solitude while she stepped between her folks. Both parents embraced her joyfully. Smiles swept their faces.

The song, "Do You Hear What I Hear," lifted the steam from their voices. She turned, watching Brian crouch on the steps of a clothing stare. Tugging on her father's pants, she whispered in his ear. A moment later, her father crossed the street.

Exhausted, hungry, and cold, Brian rested his head in his palms, mesmerized by his tears melting tunnels into the banked snow. Impatient, the runt stirred again. Brian arranged another piece of candy before the pup's nose.

As the girl's father approached, he recognized the boy. He bellowed, "Ho, ho, ho, Brian!"

Astonished, Brian raised his head. The man who played Santa Claus in the department store stood before him. The man chuckled with a victorious glow. Sitting beside the boy, he said. "I **bet** you are short one Christmas in a warm home."

Remembering his earlier wager with Santa before he fled, Brian issued a simple smile and surrendered, "Yeah, I am."

"Come home with us. We'd enjoy having you as our guest for Christmas." He extended his hand in invitation.

Cautiously as not to disturb his hand, he stood. "Do you really mean it?"

"Of course. After all, you did want 'happiness' for Christmas."

As Brian entered Santa's family home, chimes signaled the midnight hour. Entering the living room, he froze in the presence of an ornate pine tree branches stretched like arms shadowing gifts reflecting the lights from above.

Santa's wife delivered hot chocolate on coasters with a bag of mini-marshmallows tucked under her arm. "Please make yourself comfortable and add as many marshmallows as you would like." She offered to take his coat, but the boy clutched it tightly.

Giggling with excitement, his new friend informed him of the family ritual. "It's traditional to open our gifts under the tree's lights, only!"

Absorbed in the moment's ambiance, Brian watched her parcel gifts. Colorful paper and cartoon newsprint littered the floor. A single light cast an evening hue over a dedicated Nativity scene orchestrated on a bookshelf. Grateful for their kindness and generosity, Brian had no gift for them. He could give them his puppy, but who'd want a mangy half-dead pup? *He did! Both were homeless. He loved the orphan.*

The refugee observed the family immersed in paper, gifts, and laughter. Santa paused to ponder thoughts at the base of the beautiful tree. Brian reached into his coat and presented his friend.

"Here, I brought him for you. Thank you for bringing me into your home on this Christmas night."

Tears of joy rolled across his red cheeks as the family quickly gathered around the puppy. The cut on the puppy's hind side had healed and his skinny sides were full.

Merry Christmas © 1978
written by Tim Morrison

Dedicated to my three wonderful sisters, Jody, Sharon, and Diana. I'll always love you!

The Great Christmas Artist

When you love or when somebody loves you, you create a masterpiece for the entire world.

"Come on, Doc, you can't move Margaret. She means everything to Joey." The husky Dutchman pried, "Why are you moving her? Give me one good reason." His blue eyes fired a warning glance opposed to excuses.

Dr. Johnson resigned setting his medical charts on the counter as if establishing a definitive line.

""Homer, Joey's condition is not improving. You know he can't lift his head. If the slightest amount of weight is placed in his hands, he can't curl his wrists. His muscles have deteriorated to a sack of potatoes."

"Margaret is eighty-four. She's lived an extensive life. But she will not outlast Joey. I'm not sure Joey understands what death is about. I don't want Margaret to frighten him. Depression will not only sink his spirit, but will strangle his immune system."

Homer's face flushed complementing his red beard. "You separate them now; you'll surely sink Joey's ship." The muscular woodworker defended, "She needs Joey to move on in her life. Joey needs Margaret to hold his hand to help him believe he can get better. She has all the love in the world for him. She's his grandmother. She'll cradle him *forever* and that's something neither of us can do."

He seized the medical specialist's eyes with his plea.

Approaching the floor supervisor, the balding team leader rubbed his chin gingerly. "I've decided to leave Margaret Faria where she is. Contact me of significant changes."

The nurse acknowledged his instructions and issued the order.

Homer nodded. His face beamed graciously. "Thanks, Doc."

Three days before Christmas framed Pagosa Springs. It was a most unusual winter. No snow had fallen in the southern Colorado valley. Frozen tidal waves of drifted snow engulfed the high mountain ridgeline, but nature failed to serve Homer's purpose.

Blinking lights circling a Christmas tree anchored in a windowsill scattered colorful rays on the room framing the end of the hall. Homer's broad shoulders filled the doorway as he quietly slipped into the compact room. Both Margaret and Joey slept among numeric instrumentation and vines of intravenous tubing. He studied their tranquil faces ignoring the artificial support. He affirmed his conviction. "You were made for each other."

Relaxing in the rocking chair he'd brought from home, he leaned back and stared into the sun blazing below the peaks. A high cloudbank mounted their jagged edges as if to storm the valley at dawn. Homer recalled a time when Joey created a collage of pictures with construction paper frames and excessive glue. His memory quickly rewound four years of history with his son.

"What a pair," he chuckled to himself as the father of a son who had traveled so far, "to come together across the great ocean."

Joey, no more than two, arrived with boat people from Vietnam. A woman beyond child bearing years cared for Joey during the hazardous journey. Having two children of her own, she lacked the resources to rear a third. Joey's mother, like many with her, died of malnutrition and desperation. Her body was buried, perhaps "discarded" at sea. Seventeen of the original forty-three survived the ocean's torments to behold the peaceful shores of California.

The boy's blistered skin stretched tightly over his ribs. His weathered face pocked with sores. If it had not been for the immediate medical attention, he, too, might have perished with his mother to the depths of the Pacific.

Federal agencies intercepted the orphaned refugees providing avenues for adoption. Homer, thirty-seven and single, probably would have never known of Joey except for rumors rippling through the temporary refuge buildings he was contracted to construct.

In a disposable society, he enjoyed his trade as a craftsman and carpenter, building structures to shelter and protect.

The Dutchman fulfilled dreams he'd had as an apprentice under his father in Holland. His rough hands created artistic details transforming wood into elegant cabinets. At the conclusion of each, he packed his tools, inhaled the fresh air, and washed the day's exhaustion from his face.

He loved children and without much celebration he chose Joey to be his son. Initially, Joey was very frightened and reclusive. Homer spent months teaching his son to speak, draw, and play. Eventually, Homer's love and patience spanned Joey's distant island. He regretted the agony Joey might suffer some day, upon learning of his mother's death and the questionable information of his past. But with each passing struggle, the family tree became less and less important.

Enduring his second year battling multiple sclerosis, Joey had grown accustomed to hospitals. Unfortunately, Homer feared St. Luke's might be his last. Pneumonia persistently struck his son. For two summers, Joey had been confined to a wheelchair. Always seeking to improve Joey's breathing and activity, Dr. Johnson spoke favorably while his assessment grew disheartening. Homer could see it. As Joey's muscles deteriorated, he succumbed to fatigue, sleeping more and more.

On the other hand, Homer slept like the parent of a newborn, always alert at the slightest sound or movement to be present to Joey. "I wish it would snow." Homer diverted his thoughts as his eyes chased a pair of headlights in the emptying avenue below.

An enormous, frozen park enticed the Dutchman's trance. Joey wished for snow. He wanted a Christmas with snow. He'd seen numerous pictures of snowmen, sledding, and snowball fights, but he never had played in the white powder.

While meeting the requirements for constructive medical attention, Homer relocated in the Springs hoping to fulfill his son's desire to play in the powder. Framing condominiums was satisfactory, but did not complement the character the carpenter built into a home. He moved to a place where he thought they would be assured of snow, but there were serious doubts Joey would play in it.

I should have returned to Holland," he scolded, slightly louder than he intended.

"What did you say, Homer?" piped the elderly woman. Margaret's voice startled him. "Oh," she smiled, "you look like a big teddy bear lounging in the rocker."

Homer knelt on one knee and begged for her pardon. "I'm so sorry, Margaret. I didn't mean to wake you."

He sandwiched her hand between his. He figured he might extrapolate her history in the lines decorating her skin. Scars and sunspots marked her journey. "Yes, indeed," he thought, "she has led a fine life."

She laughed in the choppy manner of a woman old enough to be Homer's great grandmother.

Margaret simply had a tired body. After eighty-four years, her parts were worn. Doctors had charts scribbled with ailments and only a line or two to delay nature's inevitable course.

Blessed with two children, Margaret and her husband built a home working timber for the National Forestry Service. After militia during the Second World War claimed the life of her husband in southern Germany, she concentrated her efforts on the children. Her son settled in Boston with his family of four. Homer did not think Margaret told him of her poor health. The daughter, an aspiring executive for an influential finance company in Houston, rarely contacted her mother except to manage her financial care. Margaret remained self-sufficient. She didn't want to burden anyone. Whether right or wrong, her children were immersed in their lives.

Margaret's desire to see her little roommate's recovery gave her purpose. Joey brightened her day during a time her health was unlikely to improve. In faith, she affectionately referred to the good Lord as her Grand Papa when she talked with little ones. For reasons she understood, Joey knew she would die sometime, but not relative to his own departure. She offered Homer a certain peace about Joey's condition, which he would never muster independently.

"Are you in pain?" the craftsman questioned sensitive to interrupting her peace.

"Not really," she cleared her throat grateful for his presence. "I'm ready. The good Lord's been wonderful to me. Oh," she sighed, "we've had our discouraging moments, but overall, I've been most richly blessed."

He leaned forward and kissed her forehead.

"Did Joey tell you what he is going to be when he grows up?" A cunning glimmer lit her eyes.

"He told me he wanted to be a carpenter," Homer answered in defense of his trade.

Grinning, she rolled her eyes, "Ask him when he awakes."

"Alright?" he nodded encouraging her mischievous pleasure.

"Homer . . . would you do me a big, big favor?"

He laughed enjoying the moment. "Well, I don't know," he whispered, expecting to retrieve a glass of water. "It depends on how big. I think you've been meddling with Joey's future," he joked.

"It's bigger than you can stand. You move for all three of us."

"Count it done."

"I'm wearing a medal around my neck. The nurses wanted to take it off, but I told them, you know what . . ." She released a threatening tone. "It's a Saint Bernadette's medal. I've had it since I was a girl. I want to give it to Joey for Christmas. I really, really do," she pleaded. "Would you please take it off and put it where you'll never, ever, ever lose it. And on Christmas Eve, would you give it to Joey, please."

Homer never saw a more determined expression cross the woman's face. Her spirited brown eyes chased fatigue, encouraging strength.

"I'd love to." He smiled as if he accepted the most important task in his life. He assisted her in gently removing the medal.

As he slid the tiny silver disc into his pocket, Joey broke from his sleep.

"Well, well," Homer bellowed, "the prince has arisen." He strolled alongside the bed. Carefully, weaving between the tubes, he embraced his son. The six-year-old's smooth, tender cheeks radiated light around his sunken chestnut eyes.

"Did you have a good dream?" Homer asked.

"Nope, didn't sleep long enough. Besides, I don't dream in the afternoon."

"Oh, uh . . . Margaret told me you might have changed your mind about being a carpenter?" He hinted at a question.

"Yup, Dad, I want to be a doctor."

"A doctor?"

"Yeah and . . . a bus driver." His insight lit a spark.

"Doctors don't drive buses."

"I have to drive a bus so I can pick up sick people."

"I see. You want to be an ambulance driver," Homer assimilated.

Shaking her head, Margaret burst chuckling, "Nope."

"No, Dad! How can I fit very many people in an ambulance? With a bus, I can doctor many people. Lots of 'em!" Joey proclaimed.

Homer laughed approvingly. "That's an excellent idea. I'll tell you what, I'll mention your plans to Dr. Johnson, so he can get things lined up for you."

"You will?"

"Sure, he will," Margaret reassured.

As the evening passed, Margaret and Homer exchanged humorous childhood stories, while young Joey's laughter mended his heart. Shortly following a nurse's periodic check, Joey and Margaret drifted to sleep. Tucking each securely, he kissed each goodnight.

"Where does the time go?" Homer whispered to himself.

"Mr. Dledrich, it's five-thirty, now," a familiar voice cautioned.

Homer replied sheepishly. "Thank you."

A brilliant sun would soon dawn a new day. Rising from the rocker, he slipped into his boots, laced them, and quietly vacated the room. He would return after work in the early evening.

"Margaret, I don't want you to go." Joey pouted. "Why *do* people have to die?"

"Dying isn't bad, Joey," Margaret gathered strength from her anxiety in faith to settle his. "There was a man named Jesus who was born on Christmas. He was God's only Son. He was a person just like you and me. God sent Jesus to the people, you and me, to tell everyone, that when you die, you go to meet God. He opens the best home in all the universe for you to live. God made everything."

"No, he didn't," Joey interrupted sternly. "Dad builds homes, not God."

"God builds homes. He just doesn't build them here. He lives in Heaven. It's a magnificent, enchanted place."

"How do you know?"

"Because Jesus, His Son, told us."

"Oh."

"God especially *loves* kids," grandmother emphasized to ease the child's fears.

"He does?"

"Yes."

"As much as Dad does?"

"More than Dad does!"

"Wow!" he exclaimed innocently. "How does God decide when it's time to go?"

"Well . . . I'm not sure, but my grandmother told me a story once. I think it's *very true.*"

Patiently, Joey waited in silence as Margaret organized her recollection.

"God is a great, great, great artist and creator. Did you know he made both of us *and* everybody else out of nothing? He breathed life into dirt. People become something forever. Everybody is different. Everybody is a masterpiece. Do you know what makes a masterpiece, Joey?"

"What?" he pondered intently.

"Love. When you love or when somebody loves you, you create a masterpiece for the entire world. God loves you *all* the time, whether you're good or bad."

"He's kinda like Santa Claus, isn't he?" The child hoped in one he'd seen and believed.

"Yes, He is. He loves you all of the time, not just at Christmas."

Margaret paused to catch her breath.

"I love you even though you aren't feeling well. Homer loves you. That makes you a beautiful masterpiece. And no matter what, God always loves you. God wants it to be beautiful in Heaven. He wants everyone to join him. When you go to Heaven, you get to see everybody."

"Everybody who dies?" he cross-examined overwhelmed with the possibility.

"Yes." Margaret coughed clearing her throat.

"Wow, that's a lot of people."

"Yes, it is."

"But you can't go," her roommate pleaded.

"Joey, I'll always be with you. My spirit will be like a gentle breeze always present."

"But, I won't be able to see you," he cried. Tears formed in his eyes.

"Yes, you will!" Margaret proclaimed. "When you get to the place God selected especially for you, He opens a space in the heavens and creates a brand new star of brilliant light for all the world to see. Each star is a special masterpiece painted out of more colors than your eyes can imagine."

Joey pronounced with insight. "The big stars are for big people and the little stars are for little people. So, if I would die, Dad could see I was all right at night by viewing my star. But, how would he know which star is mine?"

She spoke with confidence to calm his fear, "Homer is real smart. He'll see it. He'll show you."

"Margaret." Joey mirrored his grandmother's eyes enveloping his in love. He sought to imprint them forever in his mind.

"Yes, dear."

"I want you to know you're a masterpiece. 'cause Dad and I both love you more than anything in the whole world."

Tears soothed her eyes. Her spirit swelled with courage, an inner peace. She needed those words to penetrate her soul.

"Margaret." Joey commanded her attention.

"Yes."

"And I'll look for your star. I'll never lose it."

She smiled pleasantly, "I know you will, Joey."

"And the angel said to the shepherds: 'You have nothing to fear! I come to proclaim good news to you—tidings of great joy to be shared by the whole people. This day in David's city a Savior has been born to you, the Messiah and Lord. Let this be a sign to you: in a manger you will find an infant wrapped in swaddling clothes.' Suddenly, there was with the angel a multitude of heavenly hosts, praising God and saying, 'Glory to God in high heaven, peace on earth to those on whom his favor rests.'"

Gently closing the book, Homer rose from the rocker. He kissed Joey, already sleeping, on the forehead.

Kneeling beside Margaret's bed, he whispered, "He tried so hard to stay awake." His red beard filled his dimples.

She smiled pleasantly. "I enjoy the story every time I hear it."

"You better get some rest." He kissed her. "Goodnight. I love you."

"And I you."

Homer wiped each carving tool clean and slid them into individual sleeves. He rolled the collection, bundling them on the maple bench. He skillfully applied protective urethane coats over Margaret's plaque. He held it proudly before him.

Decorative Rocky Mountain flowers framed the words, "Merry Christmas, Grandmother! Love always, Joey and Homer."

He chuckled, pleased with his surprise.

As he hiked across the vacant lot to his truck, he double-checked to insure Margaret's gift for Joey.

"Ready," he yelled for everyone to hear.

He felt the cold slap his face with flakes falling by the millions from above. "Oh, Joey, just wait . . . just wait! Have I got a surprise for you!"

Hiding the package beneath his coat, Homer decked the halls with joyous tunes as he sauntered between nurses rolling service carts into rooms.

"Mr. Dledrich, Dr. Johnson asked for a few minutes to speak with you." Her roaming eyes and urgency to reach the nurses' dock emphasized trouble.

"It's Joey!" Panic pumped through his chest.

"No, it's not Joey." She attempted to reassure him.

"Homer." Dr. Johnson startled the carpenter. Joyful guests carrying gifts passed as Homer ignored them.

"Please." Dr. Johnson escorted Homer away from traffic into an office.

Facing the Dutchman, the physician humbly informed, "Mrs. Faria died this afternoon."

"Margaret?" Homer battled his tears. His eyes searched the room for something unknown, but significant to him. How could he fix his absence? He assumed his presence. He had hoped to cradle her into the next life.

"She died about three o'clock. We phoned your house, shop, and construction site, but evidently we just missed you."

Though a simple fact of life, death was complicated. Nervously, Dr. Johnson cleared his throat while Homer stood suspended in time.

Dr. Johnson squeezed the carpenter's shoulder. "Homer . . . we haven't been able to wake Joey. His vitals have diminished, but stabilized." Inhaling, he continued, "I'm sorry. We've done everything possible, now we must wait. I am really sorry."

Dismayed, a father relied on senses to direct him to his son.

Homer expected machines with tubes and electrodes monitoring a woman anticipating Christmas. He settled the gift-wrapped plaque on a sterile bed with linens and blankets tucked firmly beneath the mattress.

Nestled on the broad windowsill, Homer studied the park bordering the colorfully decorated avenue. Heavy snow accumulated while a coma buried his son. Memories of Joey racing to drive nails with an oversized hammer and his jubilation that followed overwhelmed the carpenter. A deafening silence forced an antagonizing ring in his ears.

"Joey always wanted to see snow. He can't die now. He always wanted to see snow."

Unable to complete a memory, he extended his hand to the Unknown hoping to grasp an invisible line holding a precious life from sliding away. Life as a father teetered on the cliff's edge as his son's life eroded beneath him.

He knelt beside his son's bed like he had done each night to give thanks and to request healing and guidance. Holding his large hands open, he clasped Joey's small silky palm between his. Tears rolled over his cheeks. To the point of exhaustion, Homer released his spirit.

"I do not understand. I beg of You . . . please."

Leaning forward, he whispered into his son's ear. "Joey, I love you. I am not ready. It's Christmas. You can't leave me. You're my only family." He buried his face in the child's side. "Oh, Lord, please."

Homer sifted his imagination with a faint: "dad." His eyes embraced his son's. Warmth consumed him.

"Dad."

"I'm right here, Joey." He grasped his son's hands and anxiously reinforced, "I'm right here."

"Dad . . . Margaret's . . ." He swallowed.

Homer sheltered his son tightly against his chest. "I know, Joey, I know," he whispered as he ran his fingers through the boy's jet-black hair.

"Hey . . . hey . . ." he hummed as if his grandmother reminded him. "Margaret left you a present."

Homer frantically dug into his pocket, pulling forth the medal and chain. He tenderly clasped it around Joey's neck.

The boy hardly noticed the silver disk.

"It's from Margaret, Joey! Don't you like it?"

Panic seized the boy to fulfill his promise. "Dad, I want to go outside," he begged desperately.

"It's cold out there, but . . ."

Stripping the bed, Homer wrapped his son in blankets and cradled him. The lack of structure in a burlap bag of potatoes remained.

Lifting him to the window, Homer cited joyfully, "It's snow . . ." He paused. The exquisite floating flakes of moments before had ceased to fall.

"Dad!" he demanded, "I want to go outside! I have to see the sky. *Please,* Dad, *please."* Joey started crying.

"But, it's cold out there," a responsible father attempted to reason.

"Hurry, Dad, I want to see Margaret's star. Hurry!"

Without further questioning, the Dutchman bolted from the room, like a mother bear protecting young. Without a coat, he secured his son close to his chest.

"Hurry, Dad, hurry!" Joey cried. Patience lost relevance.

Bypassing the elevator, Homer rambled down the emergency stairs dropping them two at a time.

"Hurry, Dad!"

Homer burst, "I'm going fast, Joey! I'm going fast!"

Ramming his huge muscular shoulder into the last metal door between him and nature's berth, the burly father slid across the icy pavement and romped into the soft white powdered park. Upon reaching a clearing, he stopped frozen in the eve of Christmas.

"Is this good, son? Is this okay?" His position necessitated approval.

Joey didn't answer. He scrutinized the sky. Oblivious to the frigid air piercing him, he faithfully watched. Trees encompassed them, spreading their branches heralding the heavens. The lights reflected a faint orange glow off clouds settled on the horizon. It appeared it could snow at any instant. Throughout the park, darkness succeeded its throne.

Interrupting the silence, Homer spoke solemnly. "Joey . . . there aren't any stars out, tonight."

Joey struggled to speak. "I promised Margaret I'd watch for her star. She told me you'd show it to me."

Anxiety and surprise showered him. "A star," Homer mumbled nervously, "a star."

He searched the sky. "Come on, God, I need a star. I need a star."

As they attended the heavens, gentle breezes began to shift. Branches clicked in syncopation. Undaunted, the boy carefully studied the clouds.

The pale glow began to curl like the peaceful waves of an ocean. The clouds slowly commenced to open a minor clearing. The breeze swept away a thin haze.

"There's a little star, Joey!" Homer proclaimed. Rising to his toes, he lifted his son to his shoulders as if that might improve his view. "There's another star."

Joey watched silently.

Growing weary, Homer cradled his son once again. He signaled for a response. "It's a star, son. It is a star."

More distant stars appeared. In a final instant, nature gasped her last breath. Then . . . suddenly . . . with a graceful swirl, a large cloud hurled just a fraction, unveiling a bold, brilliant star gleaming in the night.

"There's her star. She's arrived, Dad. Margaret is home. *That's her star!"*

Rays scattered throughout the valley, illuminating the night sky for all to see in its vast splendor.

Life surged through Joey's limbs. "Dad, I can feel! I can lift my arms." Though not completely, he raised his skinny arms toward his favorite Dutchman.

"Let me down! I feel my legs!"

Homer succumbed to his son's plea. Intently, Joey stiffened his legs enough for Homer to insert them into the deep snow. The patient exercised a generous twist at the waist.

Awkwardly swatting snow with a bare palm, Joey sprayed his father with powder. Tears of elation melted ice crystallized to his face.

Homer released his child into snow compressed as a recliner as Joey targeted him with more snow. Snow flew everywhere as Homer tumbled in delight. Laughter echoed from their jubilance.

Yes, the greatest Artist created a new masterpiece, giving birth to new life and fulfilling the good news a Babe once proclaimed on the first Christmas Eve.

Dedicated to a special star in my life, Great Aunt Mary Budke.

Return of the Spirit

Ever so gently as if it might scar, he wiped her soft skin with his fingers, erasing his words in her tears.

"Only one week remains before Christmas. Go home, Laura," Mickie pleaded as she thumbed through a sale rack of shopper's rejects.

"How many times do I have to tell you, it just won't work," Laura scolded. "My parents wouldn't understand. I can still hear Dad lecturing me when I was fifteen. I wore a tank top I knew was revealing, but all the girls wore them. I left the house to join my friends. His words still sting. 'If you're ever pregnant without the gold band around your finger, don't expect to live off us.'"

Returning a gaudy sweatshirt scribbled in sequins, Mickie chuckled. "What girl hasn't heard their parents threaten that? They don't mean it. It's the proverbial scare tactic to prevent you from getting into trouble."

Laura tossed her brunette curls over her shoulder. Her sky blue eyes swelled. "Their words were more than a threat. You've never met them. They're proud. By coming to Atlanta, I saved them tremendous embarrassment, not to mention, my own."

"This place needs to donate this rack." Mickie abruptly concluded her browsing along with the topic.

Secular Christmas tunes and jolly St. Nick showered them. Laura trailed her closest friend out Macy's department store. They met in Atlanta at a creative advertising upstart. Laura had been hired as a temporary tech in Mickie's graphics studio.

"I'm glad we're out of there. I hate being in a place where I feel I must pay just to browse."

"The way chips fall now, you can't afford much of anything," the young advertising artist reiterated like a financial analyst.

A moist, cool breeze swept through the canyons of downtown Atlanta. Tinsel framed every showcase reflecting yellow, green, blue, red, and orange lights across the plaza. With little resemblance to life, plastic foliage imitated the Northern pines. Marquees flashed their season's greetings to spend.

"There are quaint French pastries around the corner," Mickie directed. "It's a pleasant place with light meals. My treat."

"Before Miss Colvin could excuse herself, Mickie clutched her by the arm.

Rich green plants hung from huge oak crossbeams. Laura inhaled the bread's aromas dancing around the candlelight.

Mickie interrupted her peace. "I heard eight inches of snow buried the Springs the other night.

Laura laughed nervously wiping her palms on her jeans. "What are you, a meteorologist?"

"No dummy, I read it in the national weather report in the paper."

The fruit drink tickled her cheeks. Laura studied her fingers as if there was some history or mystery behind them.

"You don't have to worry. Dishpan hands don't set in at twenty-three," Mickie joked. "You're still beautiful."

"I'm not worried," she smiled as her eyes fixed on a French tapestry hanging on the wall. "I wasn't even thinking about that." The flame lightened her blue iris and cast a warm hue upon her supple cheeks. "They don't start at twenty-five either, do they?" she poked her elder.

Miss Borgio displayed her sporty dimples. Both simultaneously stirred their crushed ice in their tropical slush. A white envelope impinged Laura's sight.

"It's a tad early, but I thought I'd better give you your Christmas present, now."

A shy grin creased her lips. "You don't want me to wait until Christmas?"

"I can't keep a surprise very long."

Tearing the edge, she pinched a pocket and pulled forth a ticket.

"An airline ticket to Colorado Springs!"

Laura's crystal blues melted with the wax. Dropping her forehead, she ran her fingers through her hair.

"You don't seem to understand. I can't go home. You don't know the embarrassment, the pain, the anguish. I'm the oldest. The oldest doesn't make this mistake."

"Read that in some magazine? The oldest does make mistakes and will continue to do so."

"They're also leaders . . . Who are you . . . my mother?"

"I'm a concerned friend. You have a baby boy reared by tenants in a low-income apartment complex. You lead your family and friends to believe you're the budding accountant you could be, but you don't have the time or money to settle down. You hardly have time for activities with your son. You live as a fictional character. Paranoid, you live in fear someone is going to break your trust."

"Go home, Laura. Take Spark with you. He's an adorable boy. Your situation may be new to them, but your parents and friends will adjust. I know by the fondness in which you talk about them."

Ms. Colvin desired a rebuttal, but their waitress interrupted. Closing the meal's formalities, both exited together.

Mickie parked at the base of the yellowing four story housing development. Wash hung to dry over several of the wrought iron balconies. The burnt red brick absorbed smog and hosted mold, revealing hazards of an inner city. The bright moon cast its reflection across the shimmering hood of her sporty sedan.

"You can't afford these," Laura resurrected the debate, flexing the airline tickets between her fingers. "I can't go home . . . I'm . . . not going."

"Wrong. I can afford these," Ms. Borgio retorted. "And you are going home. You owe it to yourself, your parents, and most of all, to Sparky."

Mickie snatched the tickets and slid them into Laura's handbag. "Besides, they're non-refundable."

Opening the door, Laura cleared her throat. "I don't think I'm going. Thanks for supper. I'll catch you later, Mick."

She didn't owe anyone anything. Sparky was too young to know better.

Tracing the headlights, the young mother entered the main hallway and climbed the hollow flight to the third floor. She eased along the harvest colored walls to Mrs. Jacob's door, wide open as always, and collecting heat from the hallway.

"Peaking around the corner, Laura captured old man Ness asleep in a stationary rocker. Ten-month-old Sparky burrowed beneath his elder's forearms, nestling against his engineering overalls.

"Oh my . . ." Mrs. Jacobs jumped. "You startled me. I didn't expect you home so soon."

"It looks as if Sparky exhausted Henry this evening." Laura grinned affectionately.

Henry's white hair crowned his baldhead. Stubble covered his chin. The skin beneath his eyes fell like drapes across his cheeks. His neck was long, thin, and straight. Snoring rumbled over the infant's silky, sandy colored hair.

"I think they tired each other," Mrs. Jacob's chuckled as she gently settled a dried plate in the cupboard. "Henry treats Spark like his own grandson. It's amazing how well they get along. Henry kept hiding homemade cookies for him all night. The little tyke is sharp and ooh . . . so observant."

"Did he eat well, tonight?"

"Like a regular butterball."

Although burglars occasionally harassed the residents, the community formed pockets of kindness, friendship, and trust. Third floor residents bonded in generosity despite Ms. Colvin's initial isolation and independence.

About ten years Henry's junior, Mrs. Jacobs formally retired from forty years as a seamstress. She craftily worked her knitting needles between her smooth soft fingers. Streaking grey laced her dark hair complementing her silver eyeglasses. Her short stubby nose characterized much of her entire body. Widowed for several years, she had seen many tenants come and go. Financially prohibited from attending college, her patience and creativity ranked her among the best in childcare.

"Mrs. Jacobs?" Laura began always with the highest respect for her elder, "I need to visit with you about something important." Laura hesitated.

"Will I lose focus of this work with this topic?" She questioned never glancing from her knitting.

"What do you think about my returning to Colorado to see my family?" Laura's pacific blue eyes glanced at the relaxed Mr. Ness.

"I don't know." Mrs. Jacobs deposited her craft in a sewing chest. "Is this a holiday visit or an extended venture?"

"I'm not really sure. I haven't made any decisions. Mickie gave me an airline ticket to Colorado Springs for Christmas. I'm insecure thinking I should go. However, this might be the time." Her heart raced the words pursing her lips."

"I think if I were a grandmother, I would like to know my grandson," she stated as if it was human nature.

"But in my case, they wouldn't necessarily know I had a grandchild if no one told them."

"Honey, I think they deserve to meet Sparky, know and feel his presence."

Henry's snore rustled the toddler, but Sparky nestled even tighter to his keeper.

Laura built her defense. "There are few places, let alone a floor of an urban complex, much like this, if anywhere in Atlanta. We have the privilege of leaving our doors open and walking freely down the hallway."

"You know . . .," Her elder returned to weaving the needles. "It wasn't like this before you came, but that is not to say it couldn't have been peaceful without you." She recalled. "When we watched you move in like you were settling for a night's stay in a motel, we knew you were in trouble. You had no furniture, just a sleeping bag. Within a few weeks, we discovered you had more than you could handle. Not only were you potential prey for some psycho, your pregnancy began to show."

"Many of us wanted to lend a hand, but we'd almost forgotten how to act," Mrs. Jacobs chuckled.

"I remember the first time we met when you brought chicken-noodle soup. I must have been about seven months, then." The memory painted a smile to Laura's peaceful features.

"Your struggle opened the doors to our own. We had shut ourselves off to those around us, those who are friends today."

Setting her knitting aside, Mrs. Jacobs weaved between a stuffed clown and foam blocks into the kitchen. In silent contemplation, Laura searched the maze of city lights. Sipping a cup of hot tea, her caring mentor continued.

"We waited anxiously anticipating Sparky's birth. A common concern bonded our generosities giving birth to new friends. Strangers spoke to me for the first time."

Her smile squeezed her wide eyes to slits.

"It was as if Spark had been born to us all."

Her plump stomach bobbled as she laughed. "When you were off on one of your assignments, people gathered where Spark crawled. His nickname formed in our minds, because of the shot he gave each of us."

"When life beats me up, I gaze into that little one's eyes and share the joy in the simple things life brings. Yes." Her chest heaved in a jovial manner. "He's our little Sparky."

Days passed quickly. Time forced the decision toward her. If there had been no deadline, Laura might have drawn a stalemate. Mickie had flown to Houston for the week, due to return Christmas Eve.

Laura's creativity wandered farther away the closer the holiday approached. Laughter echoed along the hallway.

"Sparky . . . is that good?"

"Mrs. Jacobs." She heard a sigh. "He just slobbers mush all over the place."

"He wants to play in that bowl."

Another exclaimed, "Let's get him a bigger one!"

"Now, now," Mrs. Jacobs intervened. "He's just fine. Why don't you get a warm rag and clean his cheeks?"

The toddler pounded the baby food jar with his spoon. His blue eyes swelled when his mother entered the room. A broad smile dimpled his cheeks. His stubby legs fluttered on top his high chair.

"What do you say, Sparky," she cooed, "Talk to me."

His tiny tongue lapped his lips as he gurgled gleefully.

His mother coaxed him as he rocked excitedly.

She accepted the warm cloth from the child. She methodically erased the mess from chin to forehead. Clasping his pudgy sides, Laura lifted her son from his chair. Raising him to her lips, she imprinted a smudge to his cheek. "Have you been a good boy?"

"He was a stinker earlier today," a young resident replied.

"Oh, did he ever stink," added another.

"Sparky," Laura bellowed.

Mrs. Marshall entered the small dwelling.

"Hi, Laura," she greeted pleasantly. "Has the Spark been entertaining the kids, again?"

"I think it's been some of both."

The buffet cook held out her arms to receive the rambunctious babe. Bouncing him in her arms, she questioned Laura. "Have you decided to go home or not?"

The answer unraveled, escaping her mouth. "I . . . I think I'm going home." A deep breath followed. And although the volume didn't diminish, silence seemed to isolate her from the others.

"Great," Mrs. Marshall embraced the gurgling boy attempting to wiggle free. "Yeah, you're going to see Grandpa and Grandma. Yeah."

With the children begging to cuddle Sparky, Laura shadowed her son's anxious eyes.

"You made a good decision, Laura. Inside, it's what's you really want," Mrs. Marshall affirmed.

"Fifteen minutes remain before boarding flight 687 Denver-Colorado Springs. Please have your boarding passes in order," blasted through the crowded terminal. People aligned like ants seeking their tunnel.

Mrs. Jacobs and Mr. Ness accompanied Ms. Colvin and her son to Hartsfield International Airport. It was as if her grandparents were escorting her to the airport following an extended summer visit.

The evening sky darkened. The temperature lingered in the mid-sixties.

Don't forget to call Mickie. Tell her I'll call from the Springs," Laura promised.

"What's your arrival time?" Henry inquired.

"About midnight . . . I guess **that's** Christmas morning, isn't it?" She giggled nervously as if time deceived her momentarily.

"Keep those coats next to your side," Mrs. Jacobs instructed. "Make sure you wrap Spark up good," she warned, poking him in the stomach. "It'll probably be snowing there."

A smile swept Sparky's face.

"Relax, Laura. Don't expect too much too soon. Give them a chance. You deserve it . . . and so do they."

The young woman dried tears swelling in her eyes with Sparky's multicolored knitted top. "I almost forgot." She displayed a long white envelope from her shoulder bag. She handed it to Mrs. Jacobs.

Her guardian opened it to find some pressed bills.

"We can't take this," Henry extended the envelope to her.

Laura blocked with her open palm. "There isn't much in it. I was saving it for a Christmas meal for our floor. I still want you to have the meal. I know mom will fix a feast."

Henry wrapped his thin, lanky arms around her. He whispered, "Come back and see us. We're going to miss you two."

Mrs. Jacobs kissed her adopted ones. "Don't be strangers."

"I'll probably be cast out. I'll be back sooner than you think!" Laura laughed chasing her emotions. She turned and checked through the security booth. Before disappearing into the terminal, she waved. She was leaving one family and traveling home to another.

Cold breezes pierced the ramp as she secured Sparky's wrap. Entering the lobby, she heard someone calling from beyond.

"Laura . . . Laura!"

Her family, parents, brother, and two sisters waved above the heads of other excited guests.

How did they discover her flight? She wanted to break the news slowly, to ease into it. Choking panic, the young mother's eyes darted to and fro for a place to hide. She strategically tucked her son between her shoulder bag and lapel to interrupt their vision of him.

They seemed to be approaching far faster than others in the terminal. Laura's pace broke as her heart thrust against her chest. She froze.

Instantly, her mother stopped. Laura's distraction failed to prevent two dark eyes peering from her bundle. Tiny mittens dangled, escaping her secrecy.

"Welcome home, Laura." Her mother spoke gently as if to ease the fears of a lost child. Surrendering her astonishment, she smiled. "Mickie wrote you'd be bringing a friend along . . . She made me laugh. I thought that it was kind of stra . . . You weren't expecting us. Mickie said you were going to need help." Laura's family quickly made sense of Mickie's awkward humor.

With a tinge of fear almost void of expression, Laura's dilated eyes intercepted her father's. A knot plugged her throat. She formed a word with her lips, but no word came forth.

"Let's see the little shaver." Laura's mother wrapped her arm around her daughter and embraced her, pulling the puffed hood away unveiling her new grandchild.

The strange faces frightened him. He rolled his head back and buried his face in his mother's chest.

"What do you think . . . of all the new faces, Sparky?" Laura naturally plunged her eyes into the bundle feeling her self-imposed disgrace before her family. Flushed red, embarrassed with the hidden betrayal of the love for her son, she responded immediately rocking him before her family.

"Sparky?" her brother chuckled in disbelief.

Sparky uncorked a patented smile.

"His name is 'David Henry.'" Laura spoke clearly. Tears flooded her eyes and rolled across her pale cheeks. Almost two years of repressed love poured forth.

"I didn't want . . . to embarrass you guys."

Wishing the words he had spoken had never been composed, Laura's father trembled, embracing her tightly as her brother and sisters circled her. Ever so gently as if it might scar, he wiped her soft skin with his fingers, erasing his words in her tears.

"Come here, Sparky." Her mother held him just like Mrs. Jacob's said she would.

Her sister promptly suggested, "Let's go home, you guys. We can fix some hot chocolate and . . . we got some major catching up to do!"

As the Blazer busted accumulating snow banks, they maneuvered along the countryside to small Bar-S ranch beyond the reach of urban sprawl. Fresh attention propelled Sparky from lap to lap.

Laura's listened while her siblings outlined their latest ventures.

Jumping from the four-wheeler, her father parceled the luggage. "You two grab Laura's bag and take it in while I park." The giggled as they marched toward the house.

Grandmother cuddled her new grandson, lagging the others. "Laura, I have something for you." Hesitation lingered in her voice. She withdrew an envelope from her coat pocket. "This is for you." She handed it to Laura.

Laura glanced at Mickie's return address.

"I meant to give it to you at the gate, but then I thought you might want to read it in private." The unexpected fell like the silence of the snow into her reality. She held her tears of joy and smiled. "I did some thinking during our drive home, this evening. I have a good idea what might be in it."

Her mother cradled her tiring love. "Let's take you inside and get you ready for bed. We have some big days ahead." She trudged inside, leaving her daughter to contemplate her friend's words.

Bright sparkling stars unlike any she saw in the city pierced the curtain of the midnight sky. Winter's cold nipped at the earth's dormant soil. The moon showered her powdery blue light upon the white fleece blanketing the surface. The

Rockies' jagged peaks crowned in reflective ivory towered into the heavens, surrounding a valley in the hands of God.

Tearing the end of the envelope, Laura unfolded the letter in the moonlight.

> Dear Laura, '85'
>
> I hope this Christmas brings renewal with your family. There is no way to say this delicately. Your parents are also my parents. I am your full-blooded sister. There was no way they were going to make it with me. Even though they weren't married at the time, your parents loved me and one another enough to allow me to flourish in a loving family. I'm sure an explanation is coming with Sparky and all.
>
> A child can bring much joy into the world. His simplicity and unconditional love are what our world needs to be refreshed and revived. The Christmas present isn't yours. They gave me new life. I'm simply returning their loved daughter. I love you very, very much, Laura. May God bless you.
>
> Love,
> Your sister, Mickie

Tears graced her smile as she looked ahead.

Merry Christmas © 1985
written by Tim Morrison

Dedicated to all unwed mothers and fathers whose struggles are never ignored in your children's eyes or in those of the Creator.

Fourth Down and Tomorrow to Go

Gingerly bending to gather the pieces he couldn't reach, he paused as an unusual pair of legs captured his attention. He hesitated to look up. One was real. One was not.

"It's a loss of five on the play. Spot the ball on the Denver seven, bringing up a third and goal. Only three seconds remain in the season for one of these teams while a first-class ticket to the AFC Championship awaits the victor."

"This will be the final play for Coach Brikes and the Warriors, trailing by 4, 21-17. I don't understand that call. They had the opportunity to hammer it in from the one and elected to throw the ball . . ."

"Mike, I understand some of Coach Brike's dilemma. If they failed to muscle the ball in, with no 'timeouts remaining, the clock would have expired on that play and this game would be in the annals of history. The incomplete pass stopped the clock to give them one more opportunity." The analyst complimented, "You're gambling with a stingy defense who'd just as soon bury you as look at you. Nobody plays this game for free."

"Cannon returns to the huddle with the decision . . ."

"Pro left, dubs x-y, cross dump, on three. Ready?"

"Break," the huddle burst with Marine precision.

Oscar Sanchez, the sure handed tight end broke the circle determined to release from the line of scrimmage.

"This game marks the farthest this Santa Fe expansion club has ever advanced since its introduction to the league four years ago. Three ticks separate this team from a date with Miami for the jeweled crown of the AFC."

Cheering drowned the competitors in a deafening sea of chaos. Sanchez positioned himself with an angled visual to the snap of the ball. The blaring crowd isolated him among his teammates. Breaths of steam lifted between the muscular canyons of flesh.

"Down . . . set . . ." The tailback stepped back into alignment stacked behind the fullback."

The middle backer shouted caution to his left. "Switch, Simonson left!"

"Watch Sanchez, short waggle! Blast off tackle!" Another warned.

"Hit, hit, hit."

Oscar watched his center lunge forward delivering the ball on cue. His forward thrust undercut the heavy nose guard. Fighting to separate the defensive end clutching his jersey, Oscar uppercut the two-hundred-sixty pound lineman with a forearm, driving his head back and dodging the leg scramble. Free, he isolated on Cannon's empty hand. His eyes instinctively tracked the spiral tunneling through arms of defenders toward him like a speeding bullet. Leaping vertically, Sanchez reached for the airborne pigskin.

"What a shot! I don't know if Sanchez held on . . . The Pro-Bowl tight end was scissored just as he touched the ball."

The play-by-play announcer paused. "The officials signal. Sanchez scores! Touchdown, Santa Fe! The Warriors have a date in Miami! People are swarming the end zone, but Sanchez has not risen. He took one heck of a shot."

The ball had been taken from his side. Oscar lay on his back gasping for air. Blood seeped from his lips.

"Get back! Get back!" Teammates cordoned the area with a protective circle of arms around their clutch receiver. Pulling an oxygen tank behind them, team medical staff broke the fraternal circle.

"Take it easy Osc. We're gonna pipe ya some O-2. Get the stretcher over here," the emergency doc ordered. "We need to get him out of the weather and into the locker room."

Sunlight streaked the room, reflecting off Oscar's eyes. Blinking, he rolled his head to the right and then to the left. In one arm, a tube fed a colorless liquid from a pouch hanging above him. Another ran from the other arm to a machine with a pair of mini screens integrated with computer support systems.

Attempting to draw a deep breath from the tubes entering his nose, pain fragmented throughout his chest.

Suddenly, a gentleman in a white lab coat entered the room. "You're a hell of a receiver, Oscar," he complimented.

Oscar formed words, but the pain rudely dampened them.

"I'm sorry to bare the bad news. You **must** take it easy for a few months. You broke two ribs. Both punctured and tore a good-sized hole in your left lung. We saved as much capacity as possible, but you lost about twenty percent of your lung. As you rolled over your arms with the catch, you ripped your lung open and you began to bleed."

"I'm sure it's painful, but how **do** you feel—all things considered?" Dr. Curtis asked sympathetically as he scribbled notes to his patient's chart.

"I'll manage," Oscar whispered with a delicate swallow.

As if timing mattered, Coach Brikes barreled into the room carrying a football. "You need to quit hunting for cross-fires." Tucking the ball to Oscar's side, he celebrated, "The whole Santa Fe program thought you deserved the game ball. Sorry you're going to miss Miami, Saturday."

Oscar smiled and traced the lace and leather with his fingertips.

"Let's hope Williams can make half the plays." Coach Brikes sympathized with his disappointed tight end. "Williams was solid at UCLA, but we'll be asking a lot of a rookie. He's had little playing time."

The thought of anybody replacing him increased the intensity of pain pulsing through Oscar's limbs. Traded to his home state from Kansas City after Pro Bowl performances, Oscar, 32, always dreamed of playing in the Super Bowl.

His mother, pregnant by a derelict husband, crossed through the San Luis Pass in the Animas Mountains from Mexico into the U.S. to harvest tomatoes for the commercial growers in Gila Valley. She married one of the American rogue directors. With reservations, she led Oscar to believe this man was her real father, but as Oscar advanced through elementary school, it became apparent his skin tone was much darker with smoother facial features than his father's. Eventually, his mother revealed the truth of the man who abandoned them living somewhere in Leon. He never allowed 'step' to precede the name of the man who tossed him his first pass. His father never missed a football game. Determined to put Gila Valley on the map, Oscar dedicated himself to the organization in quest of the Super Bowl.

After mentally replaying the miracle catch, the Warriors' chief strategist wished Oscar good health and rapid recovery. The injured Warrior gazed at the burnt orange sky as the sun set behind the snow capped Sangre De Cristo Mountains.

Late afternoon the following day, nurses removed the tubes from his arms and nose and wheeled away an electronic monitor. He had his bed tilted to a slight angle such that he could enjoy his liquid diet. Flowers with 'get well' cards and humorous anecdotes from many of his teammates were delivered throughout the day.

During Dr. Curtis' final round of the day, he quizzed his patient. "How's the breathing, today? Easier, I hope."

Oscar spoke prompting a positive response. "I'm hoping I heal well enough to attend the Super Bowl in three weeks should the Warriors seal the deal."

Oscar exhaled and inhaled as directed while Dr. Curtis examined his lungs.

Prying for additional information, yet hesitant at what might be revealed, Oscar inquired, "What lasting effect will this have on my career?"

"A game of touch would be a Super challenge," the physician joked with a hint of seriousness. "At this point, it's difficult to say with any certainty. If you were not the caliber athlete you are, your professional playing career would be history. However, your skills and talent have kept you in the starting lineup . . . I do think you may view from a sky box for the Super Bowl."

"You're saying I can make up the deficit," the big tight end interrupted the specialist's examination.

"You might, but not for next season. It is not the loss of lung capacity, which is so detrimental in this instance. It is the location of the two ribs you broke. Ribs heal very slowly. The actual breaks are extremely close to cardiac muscle. Initially, before surgery, we thought a rib might have punctured one of the cardiac chambers. Severe internal bleeding made it difficult to pinpoint until we were able to clear the area."

Oscar felt he should have let the rib tear through his heart just as the surgeon's prognosis did. Nobody had to tell the All-Star his position was available. Rookie Williams knew the tight end position was his for the taking.

Desiring to share the game among loyal fans, Oscar reclined in the guest lounge at the end of the hall. He dissected the game play by play from the color monitor. The warm sun kissed the citrus state. Fans packed Dolphin Stadium for the AFC Championship game. As another Budweiser commercial interrupted play, Oscar looked to poll the Warrior fans only to discover he watched the game alone. People chose isolation over team camaraderie.

As each offensive series elapsed, Oscar's palms grew moist. His heart raced more watching the game than when he played. Adrenalin coursed through his arteries heightening his senses. The battle on the gridiron teetered back and forth.

"Come on, Cannon, throw the ball." The pass fell short and incomplete. "You're pushing it." Once again, time choked the Warriors.

The announcer reminded, "Williams has four catches on the night for . . ."

"One hundred eight yards at twenty seven yards a reception," Oscar recited as though he'd been hired to record the stats.

The predicament he discovered left him frustrated. Every scouting report in the league noted the Warrior's rallied late with their tight end in clutch situations. Should Williams make the key plays down the stretch, his confidence would soar. Coach Brikes knew, as did Oscar, that the youngster had good hands and excellent speed.

"He hasn't had much playing time . . .," echoed through Oscar's thoughts.

"It's third and about eighteen from the Warrior thirty. The clipping penalty nullifying Johnson's twelve-yard burst has set this Warrior offense back into last season. Cannon can't play the short game. He must go long to keep the drive alive."

"The snap from center, Cannon drops and guns across the middle on a fifteen yard strike to Williams. Williams is hit twice, but remains on his feet. He's beyond the first down marker tight-roping his way down the sideline for a gain of thirty seven."

"What a second effort! This may be the fundamental difference between Sanchez and Williams. Williams is about twenty pounds heavier and is more prone to break away from would be tacklers."

"Damn it, Cannon!" Oscar shouted. "Throw it to Tucker, He's wide open."

"From the Dolphin thirty seven with just under a minute to play, Cannon drops back again. Tucker slants to the middle. Williams floats to the outside. The ball's thrown to Williams. He's got it. He steps toward the sideline, and breaks deep into Dolphin territory, before being shoved out at the eleven."

Oscar studied the screen. His ears amplified the commentary. "Back to back receptions for the rookie. He's rolling up some impressive numbers, today. On consecutive plays, Cannon has gone to the Bruin out of UCLA for almost sixty yards."

Oscar watched Johnson carry the ball twice for eight yards to the three. With less than thirty seconds to play and one timeout remaining, the Warriors need six to win it. Johnson took the pitch from Cannon around the left side.

"Motte's there to make the play, giving the Warriors fourth and a foot to the Super Bowl. Santa Fe uses their final timeout. The Warriors come to the line of scrimmage. Johnson again, takes the pitch to the left side. Williams springs like a cat, trimming both Motte and Stanton. Johnson cruises into the end zone, untouched! Touchdown Warriors!"

As if Williams didn't already have a stat sheet worthy of a game ball, the injured Warrior continued to listen while he sifted the rookie's stats for the day. "Williams makes a sensational block, clearing a path to the Super Bowl!"

Throwing his arms back in frustration, one slammed against a potted poinsettia, sending it across the room. The sound of it shattering on the floor momentarily interrupted the conflict rising between his bruised ego and his desire for the Warriors to play in the Super Bowl.

Gingerly bending to gather the pieces he couldn't reach, he paused as an unusual pair of legs captured his attention. He hesitated to look up. One was real. One was not. One was scrawny and bruised with a knobby knee. One was smooth, dull, plastic, and artificially joined to the upper leg. The momentary pause consumed him.

The game announcers rattled on with closing remarks, but failed to distract the professional Warrior.

"Do you need help?" The high-pitched voice startled him forgetting an actual person might be attached to those legs.

Stealing a glance, he focused on the big brown eyes of a child.

"My name is Rebecca." She smiled extending a helping hand.

"Nice to meet you, Rebecca." He bowed to shake her hand. "I'm Oscar."

Her sparse hair, about a half-inch long, for all cosmetic purposes left her bald. A raised seam traced the back of her scalp. Gaudy jewelry draped her neck. A small purse hung from her shoulder and ruby red lipstick embellished her lips, prematurely pushing her nine years into nineteen. Her unique, noticeable features blended together to restore a form of normalcy.

Cocking her prosthetic leg slightly, she knelt to the floor on the artificial limb. With all of his size and strength, the humbled pro receiver watched her gather up most of the mess he had created.

"How long have you been here?" she asked while collecting scraps.

"Six days. I'm checking out, tomorrow. How long have you been here?"

"I live here." She spoke casually without interrupting her cleaning.

"In an apartment or something?" Oscar replied without thinking.

She lunged forward landing in a recliner. Her grand smile dropped clues. "I don't really live here, it just seems like it. But if you want to find me, look in the children's wing. I'm here most months."

"What'a ya doing on this floor?"

"Exploring. I actually know this hospital pretty well." She spoke proudly as a guide might on tour. "Lots of nurses and doctors know me."

The tight end quickly calculated the seasons he'd have lost in the company of a building full of ailing individuals.

Embarrassed, Oscar stood as a janitor walked into the room.

"Hi, Mr. Kamer." The dimples creasing her cheeks warmed his heart. "I forgot," she beamed, "I know most of the medical assistants as well."

"Did you see Santa, this morning, Rebecca?" The short, balding man in gray overalls efficiently removed a dustpan and whiskbroom from below the counter and collected the loose soil and shards of clay.

"No, the pictures they took of my head went overtime. He left me a bag of candy, though."

Her elder gently touched her cheek and gently took the broken clay from her.

"I'm sorry. I . . .," Oscar began to apologize.

"You're Sanchez, tight end, hero for the Warriors." Excited to meet the Pro-Bowler, Mr. Kamer extended his hand. "I heard you were injured, but we were strictly told not to bother you. If it ain't no bother, could you sign this pad for me? The grandsons would sure be impressed!"

Oscar graciously autographed the pad while Mr. Kamer replaced the pan and broom. Bobbing his head acknowledging gratitude, he honored the patient's privacy and entered the main corridor.

"Miss Rebecca, may I escort you . . . to wherever you want to go?" Oscar offered.

The little princess threw her pointed elbow his way. "You may, sir."

As they wandered along the hall, Oscar enjoyed the Christmas character cutouts taped to the doors. Crepe paper hung twisted from entrance to exit. A small ornate tree illuminated the end of each floor.

"So you're a professional football player." Rebecca pondered. "I don't like football much. On Saturday and Sunday, it's on all the channels and there's nothing to do around here. I think that's why they schedule my long treatment sessions. They make me sick." She grimaced, entering the children's wing of elves, angels, reindeer, and ornaments. "I'm getting kinda tired."

"Well, then, we won't talk about football. I'll put you to bed and let you rest . . . and we will talk about whatever you want."

He trailed her dodging the cane she casually tossed to the side. He lifted her to the mattress suppressing an up-thrust of pain. He eased himself into the chair beside the bed. His princess methodically laid her purse and jewelry on the nightstand. Without modesty, she stripped to her underwear and slipped into her gown printed with palominos. Reaching beneath her gown, she pulled some snaps to a hip harness and dropped the leg on the floor. Oscar stared at the artificial form expecting it to twitch with life. It warned of the fragility of his own health.

"You think you should be so rough on your leg?" Oscar studied the child's sincere distain for the limb.

"I don't like it. I ought to paint it a different color or something. They're all the same."

Neither wanted to discuss it anymore.

Rebecca nestled her pillow and charmed him with her smile. He dimmed the lights.

"You were mad, tonight," she recovered their introduction before the janitor's interruption.

"Yes, I was." He put into words what she might understand. "You know how you dream for something really grand? I told everybody back home I was going to play in the Super Bowl, the greatest game in football."

"Why can't you, someday?"

"I got hurt. When I first played for this team, our team was not very good. But over time we improved and now my team is going to play in the Super Bowl."

"Maybe you can play, next year."

"I don't think so. There is a younger player who is fast, has good hands and is bigger than me."

Lifting her head off the pillow with eyes wide open, she spoke in disbelief. "Bigger than you?"

"Yes, and he had a good game tonight. He was the hero."

"Can't you do something else?" Her voice proclaimed optimism.

Mesmerized, ideas failed to surface. "All I've ever done is play games." The conversation exhausted her as she drifted to sleep. Trivial isolation settled. Her rest in peace enveloped him in kind. Quietly, he wandered into the hall. Pausing at the nurses' station, he sought information from the evening supervisor.

"How **is** Rebecca?" There was the convenient answer, but his tone negotiated understanding of the child's condition.

"Rebecca has spinal tumors. She's been on chemotherapy for the last six months."

"What are her chances for recovery?"

"It's often a losing battle. However, that little girl has done much, much better than expected. She's ahead in the game. We're constantly monitoring her condition, taking blood samples, running MRI scans . . . At this stage, she has a better than fifty percent chance of remission."

Dr. Curtis discharged Sanchez clearing him to fly to San Diego for the Super Bowl. Coach Brikes encouraged his tight end to join the team for inspiration and to feed face time to the media. "Your presence on the sideline will inspire all the guys. Get here ASAP!" Brike's words recharged Oscar, damping the self-inflicted competition with rookie Williams. The recuperating Pro-Bowler's reunion would enhance his stock with the Warrior organization.

After collecting his personal care information, Oscar peaked into Rebecca's room. Pale, she lay in bed as a hematologist drew a blood sample from her shrinking arm.

Displeasure darkened her face with an approaching storm. "I don't feel good . . ." she sighed lifting sunken eyes to her Hispanic friend.

Cloaking her with his shadow, he kissed her forehead. "I'll return after the Super Bowl and we'll do something really fun, whatever you'd like."

A twinkle splashed his face hoping to coax a smile. She closed her eyes to sleep, failing to share his exuberance.

"Final boarding call for all passengers flying Frontier West to San Diego, Flight 117, boarding at gate 32."

With his back to the gate door and rollaway luggage against the wall, Oscar Sanchez sat inconspicuously watching jets taxi to the runway while others roared into the heavens. As the gate door slammed shut, mounted televisions were replaying highlights of his catch in Denver. Oscar's memory launched him high into the air to snatch an overthrown spiral. His Boeing 727 taxied to the runway. His heroic effort extended the Warriors' dreams. Rookie Williams starred in a game he was previously slated to watch in Miami closing the door on Oscar in Denver and opening one for himself in San Diego. The 727 rumbled down the runway thrusting skyward. The gate area silenced. The stadium emptied. Oscar sat oblivious to the other jets.

He stood to wheel his luggage behind him. He chuckled aloud, "There has to be a better pair of legs."

Wandering throughout Santa Fe collecting materials, Sanchez went to work. During the afternoon, he entered St. Francis Children's wing. Peering into Rebecca's room, he noticed a vacant bed, sheets crisply tucked and firm. The prosthetic leg lay at the foot of the bed. He inquired at the nurse's station.

"I'm sorry Mr. Sanchez. Rebecca suffered a relapse today. She's in the intensive care unit on the second floor."

Oscar felt his heart roll as his chest tightened with pain. He fought to capture a deep breath as he carried his gifts back to her room. Sweat poured off his forehead as the hot flash consumed him. He reclined in the chair to recompose.

With heavy legs, he followed directions to the ICU. His charming princess, frail and exhausted, lay hooked to cold, unresponsive machines maintaining her vital functions. Data streamed across monitors while catheters fed nutrients and antibiotics. Cupping her tiny curled fingers in the palm of his hand, he silently prayed for healing. He imagined dreams dancing in her sleep. He wanted to execute a play, perform a miracle, and make life whole for her. Anxiety swelled among the machines. Were they supporting her or slowly sucking life from her and draining those around her?

A nurse examined printed data. Oscar choked a whisper. "Is she alright?" He feared her response.

"I honestly can't say. There are days, if you didn't know any better, you'd think she belonged on a playground with all the other kids. And . . . there are days when Rebecca can't keep food down. She can't walk. Her vision, hearing diminishes. There are days like these that we can only hope and pray something . . ." Her voice rose in pitch offering the impossible may come to fruition.

Rebecca's spirit of exploration lifted him as he recalled the first instance he knelt at the foot of the artificial leg on which she stood. While cleaning up his mess, she inadvertently excused him of his private thoughts of jealousy. He recognized in her . . . his determination to win. Each game featured a winner and a loser. She played to win. Losing was not an option.

Outside, he stared into the eve of Christmas. The sun's fire brushed a red hue across the snow-covered Sangre De Cristo Mountains casting a warm glow upon the adobe city. The white jagged edges gradually surrendered to the majestic purple draped with the rays of the moon and the stars.

Christmas day surrendered to night. Staff returned Rebecca to her room where Oscar relentlessly kept watch. Believing they were the steps to heaven, he scrutinized the mountain range. Gradually, nature presented the same landscape cloaked with nature's impressive red and orange. Rebecca battled to blossom another day with the fullness of life . . . talents unexplored. He hoped this nine year old would experience sledding, birthday parties, school, horses, dates, walking, hearing, seeing . . .

Oscar fell to his knees, clasping his fingers between hers. "Lord, heal her. Make her well. She has lifted me from despair to thanksgiving for the many talents You've bestowed. I love this little girl. I know I'm asking a lot, but please let her win this one."

He felt a slight pressure on his hand. Rebecca opened her eyes, accenting a glow from her face. Tears formed in the large receiver's eyes.

"Are you sad again?" Dimples rolled into her cheeks.

"I'm very, very happy."

She frowned. "I'm sad. I still don't feel good."

"It'll come," he cheered stroking her chin. Reaching for one of the wrapped gifts, he held it before her.

Her smile flushed the gloom from her broken body. She tore into the paper revealing a mule piñata.

"It's filled with all kinds of candies and special surprises. You can break it when you're feeling up to it."

"Will you be here?"

"I wouldn't miss it," he promised, dedicating his life to her.

"You're not going to the Super Bowl?" She remembered his dream.

He laughed, "You're my best dream come true! There's no game that compares to being here with you!"

Setting the piñata aside, he delivered a small silver gift. Rebecca slowly tore the paper, revealing a maroon and white stocking cap. She studied the caption. Oscar had ripped away the 'Warriors' emblem and stitched, "Rebecca—All Pro" along the bottom. It wasn't fancy, but it was made for his best teammate. Excited to wear it, her eyes begged him to help her put it over her head.

"I thought it would keep you warm when I carried you outside to see the decorations." She lifted her arms like an infant awaiting her ride. His muscular forearms cradled her easily as he rambled out the door.

Trudging in the snow reflecting the spectral colors of lights, Rebecca quickly spied her parents anxiously standing beside a bench with a package between them.

"Mom! Dad! I told you Oscar was visiting me!" Her parents graciously huddled around their tight end to embrace their daughter as he settled her in their arms. "Santa brought you a present!" her parents exclaimed in one voice.

She held a light, almost half-moon shape gift. Wasting no time, she shred the paper to reveal the latest in prosthetic legs.

Rebecca began to cry uncontrollably. Her mother held her tightly.

"I know it's hard, sweetheart, but we **all** believe you will be well soon." The breath of her mother's faith entered her child.

Holding the polished metal sliver, Rebecca's personal Santa presented it to her to examine.

"It's titanium. It's light. It stores energy. It's ready for a little girl like you to grow into a fine young lady." Oscar embraced her, whispering, "Merry Christmas, Rebecca. Merry Christmas!"

Dedicated for all those who struggle to take a step forward each day.

Spirit of the Ukraine

There is a force beyond us, a power unmoved by weapons, and a peace no army can destroy. We must surrender what we are for what we might become.

Completing the final track exchange, the diesel engines expelled thick black smoke as they thundered out of the city of Novgorod for the northern plains of the Ukraine. A thin blanket of snow cleansed the dark polluted streets where Natasha Tatyana had played soccer as a child. Livestock speckled the surrounding landscape. A large, stern man wedged into the seat beside her breaking her trance. Her heart paused and rolled against her chest once she realized who he was. Avoiding eye contact, her palms grew moist as she dampened her breathing. Suspicion paralyzed her.

Initially, he ignored her. She hardly believed this was a coincidence.

Aware she was staring into his reflection off the window, he spoke casually without threat. "Going home to visit your aunt, Natasha?"

Even though she expected conversation, he startled her. She coughed a barely audible, "Yes."

Perceiving the youth's apprehension, he tapped the seventeen-year-old on the knee. "Relax; traveling by train is much safer than traveling by plane, more scenic." The curl in his lip revealed a gold-capped incisor. "I understand you are doing quite well at the University in Moscow, studying electrical engineering, is it?"

As if he didn't already know, she forced a smile. "Quite well, sir."

His robust frame and facial scars naturally intimidated people.

"I am returning from Chernobyl. The plant is operating efficiently, again, though not at peak with one of the reactors lost forever. Many good engineering opportunities exist in other plants across the country. With your progress and demonstrated excellence at such an early age, I think exceptional positions may be made available, provided you remain loyal to Party lines."

"I have," she quickly assured him. "I . . . I would never choose to jeopardize my career."

He glanced at the frozen farmland. Her eyes followed his. Casually dictating a threat to her future, he stated, "It's a shame . . . your grandfather . . ."

"We've never met." Her genuine honesty eased the tension, knowing where the Ukraine deputy's questions were leading.

"Do you know where he is?"

Dmitri Vorotnikov's appearance was no accident. She listened intently to the Ukraine's chief official to Moscow's Congress of People's Deputies.

"He was sentenced to serve as a physician for prisoners of war along the Afghanistan border. Do you believe justice was served?" His baited question irritated her. She sought clues to her grandfather's disappearance in the Deputy's disclosure as the locomotive rumbled toward the Ukrainian capital, Kiev.

"He publicly embarrassed our motherland, disgracing our campaign through Afghanistan with his harsh words of dissention. He even denounced your father's involvement, a decorated officer, in a war which savagely claimed his life."

The passenger car rocked back and forth, as Natasha recalled pictures of her father decorated in military green. War claimed his life shortly after he gave her a bicycle for her eleventh birthday. *Tass* proclaimed him a hero in a battle where he seized control of a strategic bridge through a mountainous region filled snipers and vast systems of tunnels. Her father's body and personal possessions were never returned.

"I don't understand your grandfather's condemnation of his own flesh and blood, simply because he supported the welfare of our nation. He speaks of our inhumane treatment of the people who deny our supply of fuel from the Persian Gulf, labeling them 'poor and illiterate'."

Dimitri effectively struck Natasha's nerve of bitterness toward her grandfather. His defiance limited her family's access to some vegetables and heating fuels during the winter. However, she chose to listen rather than respond.

"He, also, had the audacity to speak out against our educational systems, claiming we only educate the 'aligned' class." Dmitri laughed aloud squeezing her arm to insure eye contact.

She had seen condemned pictures of her grandfather removed from the Academy of Sciences Medical Institute. Regardless of the State's attempt to erase his existence, Leo Tatyana's contributions to neurology were vast and complex. His achievements challenged the finest neurologists in the world.

"There can be no God that contradicts the teaching of the State and establishes Himself superior to it. Nor will the State acknowledge individuals who teach, publish, or philosophize on such scandalous, revolutionary ideals to our people," he stated emphatically. His domineering brown eyes demanded a statement of commitment.

"I hope I never meet him. His life is nothing but paradox and contradiction, something that only stirs unrest in the hearts of good men." She felt as if she'd just testified against a criminal, for her grandfather did bring great shame to the Ukraine and to her family. After her father's death, her mother abandoned the family in its misery and sought to divorce herself from the Tatyana name. Natasha lived with her father's sister and finished her secondary education in two years in Kiev. Such acceleration was encouraged and she was immediately selected for the University of Moscow.

As the huge diesel engines billowed smoke along the reservoir damned on the Pnieper River, Dimitri unfolded some newsprint. "Your grandfather has been transferred to a labor camp in the Ukraine." A patronizing expression straightened a scar beneath his eye. "He is cutting stone in our largest limestone quarry along the Donets River in Gorlovka. His fingers may never touch another scalpel." Although the theatrics were meant to intimidate, Deputy Vorotnikov sounded almost sympathetic, considering the isolated talent.

As the train throttled down entering the depot, people quickly gathered their belongings and moved to exit. Dmitri slid into his sooty dark coat and gloves. Before leaving, he reminded, "Remember, hard work and loyalty to truth. Wash shame from the Tatyana name. Enjoy your stay."

"Thank you," she replied remaining seated.

Water sparkled like diamonds against the dark frozen soil thawing in the afternoon sun. The glistening baroque domes of St. Andrew and St. Sophia cathedrals reigned over the unusually still day across the turned fields of the Russian breadbasket. Like sixty percent of the churches converted to museums in Kiev, Percherska Lavra, once a thriving monastery symbolized the significance of religion, vacant and sterile. To publicly profess one's faith was to renounce the Communist Party and its potential benefits, jobs, promotions, medical care, and education. To instruct minors, those under twenty-one, was strictly forbidden.

With a pack over her shoulder, Natasha hiked into the Podol district, an area of Kiev's abandoned warehouses and flats. At age nine while her father served in the army, Natasha was sent to live with her aunt in a section of a district warehouse renovation. A constant flux of the young and educated migrated into the district.

As she slid over the cobblestone street beneath the huge chestnut tree she climbed as a child, Natasha heard her aunt call. The women raced into each other's embrace.

"It is great to see you!" Anna proclaimed. "Your journey was tiring?"

The fresh air and Kiev, a much more decorated urban center than Moscow, seemed to ease the burden she felt while traveling. "It was okay," her niece shrugged, "Deputy Vorotnikov rode beside me."

With guarded excitement, Anna escorted her inside. "Was he stern?"

"Not exactly. He talked of Grandpa Leo and how I must avoid his proclamations, especially if I expect to receive a strong education and solid employment."

Wrapping an apron around her waist, her aunt rattled plates onto the table. "I can understand why he might say that, after all, my father renounced the Party. We were living in a beautiful home with plenty. Then he defended those who believed in a Supreme Being, education and medical care for all, and perhaps the worst, condemned the Party's aggression toward Afghanistan." Anna carried some hot borscht to the table. "Your father died a decorated hero in that war. Your Grandpa Leo openly criticized the war shouting 'these lives are lost for the greed of a few.'" Her recitation wrinkled her brow and scattered her auburn hair.

Inhaling the rich beet aroma, Natasha seated herself and naively initiated a defense. Shouldn't medical care and education be made available to all?"

"It is," Anna stated, blowing a cooling stream across her soup. "But, not to criminals, contradicting the State. Each must carry their share of the labor and collectively support the Party. Otherwise vast inequities and chaos arise. Russia could not survive. For supporting anti-Soviet agitation and propaganda, such as promoting false freedom and human rights, these individuals have denied themselves the access to medical care and education.

The day expired with the setting sun. A bright light illuminated a quaint space for reading. The kitchen-dining room area was narrow and plain. A large upstairs bedroom sectioned by curtains complete Anna's three room portion of the warehouse. Cold breezes penetrated the cracked masonry. The borscht warmed the body. Anna finished her feast serving bleeny and straw-boiled ham with a caramel-potato tort evening surprise.

Long after Anna had retired for the evening, Natasha sat reading in bed. Glancing over the upper margin of her book, her eyes focused on a roll-top trunk. Frowning, she couldn't recall seeing it there during the summer. Setting the text aside, she tiptoed toward it and quietly rolled the lid. She discovered chronicles, pictures, and articles documenting her father's assignments. Lifting what appeared to be a common ledger, she returned to her bed. Scanning the pages, she noticed strips of paper taped to the inner margins behind the center pages. Pausing to read a couple, she recognized the salutations to her father, the text of each hand written by her grandfather Leo. Some letters were warm and compassionate, in addition to, others informing his son of the laboratory work he had performed.

"Dear Son," she read, "thousands in Moscow and across the Soviet Union are exposed to starvation, homelessness, disease, and humiliation, while I stuff myself with pork and vegetables. It is a crime against all human dignity, committed continuously; and I ignore those injustices with my convenient service to the State. Man's illness is not cured if only the symptoms are treated."

Upon reading the final entry, Natasha imagined it might have been the final correspondence a father had with his son. It was a plea for his son to consider resigning from further military service in Afghanistan.

"Dear Son, I hope this letter is not too late. I have studied many writings of a man deeply moved for peace, Tolstoy. I disagree with your philosophy . . . '*as long as violence is controlled by some disciplined party organization or national state, it is an acceptable means to a desirable end."(1)* After reading summaries of conferences hosed in Europe and the United States to promote peace, I have drawn this conclusion; the same Tolstoy drew about the meaningless slaughter of Jews at the turn of the century. These countries' governments are hypocritical; that they will constantly try to increase their military power, strangling their economies in the illusory name of peace . . . entrenched in their own rhetoric. Peace will only be achieved abroad after it is achieved at home in the caring concern for others. Peace be to you, love, Dad."

Natasha carefully tucked the personal ledger between the thin mattresses. Winter's chill submerged her beneath Aunt

Anna's down comforter. Satisfied her treasure was safe, she drifted to sleep. One week, remained before Christmas.

Natasha carried hot water from a community heater in the complex back to Anna in the kitchen. The exercise generated warmth and companionship. After washing dishes, she rinsed and hung clothes.

"Actually, Deputy Vorotnikow startled me on the train, yesterday." Natasha began to confess. "I have read some spiritual texts and excerpts from a book called the Bible."

Panic pierced her aunt's eyes. "You did not bring them into this house, did you?"

"No, no, they aren't mine." Her aunt's fear bred curiosity. "They belong to a friend. I saw pictures of cities in the United States of America decorated for Christmas. I know pockets of families in Kiev secretly celebrate Christmas. I know what Christmas is and who we honor."

"Who *you* honor!" Anna scolded in a raspy voice fearing someone might be listening.

Natasha rambled out of control. "What's wrong with sharing a spirit of generosity and of praising God?"

"You are crazy. You speak just as foolishly as your grandfather," Anna accused.

Wadding her apron and throwing it inside the door, Anna stomped from the kitchen into the street shouting, "I'm going to the market. By the time I return, **you** will have reevaluated your future career or prison."

Water trickled down the drain irritating Natasha as she watched her aunt march around the corner.

While the pair diced potatoes, Anna answered the knock at their door. Deputy Vorotnikov and three darkly dressed agents inquired. "Have you seen or heard from Leo Tatyana?" He revealed a flier of newsprint.

Anna quickly browsed the bulletin. Frowning, offended, she abruptly slapped his palm with print. Neither offered it to Natasha.

"He could not write this. He is in prison," Anna defended, exaggerating her lack of sympathy for her father.

"He has escaped the limestone quarries. This is definitely his style of writing. These are his concepts for human rights." The bitter cold never fazed the boorish Soviet leader.

"These ideas are similar, but neither of us supports beliefs contesting the Party," she testified firmly.

Intently listening, Natasha continued cutting carrots and meat for the evening stew.

"I will travel to Gorlovka and capture this revolutionary. I swear I'll send him to Siberia once he's captured. Remember, to interfere comes at a great price."

Dmitri mocked courtesy tipping his hat. He gave instructions to the agents as Anna closed the door. "Stay and watch any movement to or from the premises. If either leaves, follow them. Report to me, immediately!"

Just before sunrise, against Anna's wisdom, Natasha packed a knapsack of essentials. As the frigid wind chased one agent to break for warmth, she climbed out a blindside window and hiked to the depot. The Artic winds were relentless. Cautiously, she scrutinized the dock for anyone suspicious. Nobody appeared interested in her.

The train ride to Gorlovka went exactly as planned, uneventful. Gorlovka, a poor mining town north of Donetsk, supplied rich coal for generating electricity for much of the State.

The wind ceased. Paranoia bred insecurity as Natasha alertly searched for familiar faces around her. Not far from the train depot, she located the main entrance to the enormous limestone quarries. The workday expired. The temperature plummeted sharply with the setting sun. Capped in tattered wool and insufficient clothing, men passed single file through the gateway. Natasha reviewed the file for elders. There were few. No one matched her grandfather's description.

"Sir," she hollered running after one with a knotted gray beard and overalls.

Fatigue pressed him.

"Please . . ., I am searching for my grandfather, Leo Tatyana. I didn't see him working, here." She graciously, yet cautiously surrendered a privileged traveling visa to prove her identity.

"Put that away," he commanded nervously glancing around. Approval lit snake eyes. "I can't tell you where he is, but he is of good health. He would love to see his granddaughter."

The man stuffed his pipe and forced a couple drags. "There is a barn two kilometers from the outskirts of the city running parallel to the old coal road. He'll find you there. Remain hidden and as inconspicuous as possible."

Paranoia exhausted her as she traced her steps. Reaching the barn, the young engineering student climbed to the loft and arranged the straw to hide herself. She unpacked some ham Anna had prepared along with an apple. Quietly, she ate.

Snuggling in the hay insulating her from the northern winds, her body generated protective warmth. Fighting the rigors of travel and secrecy, she drifted to sleep.

Through the swinging loft doors, light sliced across her face. An icy breeze stung her lips. Hidden, she acclimated herself to images through straw camouflage. Her knapsack lay buried. Grandpa Leo had not shown.

"*Perhaps, I'm in the wrong barn,*" she considered a missed opportunity, "*or . . . maybe he saw someone trailing me whom I did not see.*"

Brushing herself, she climbed from the loft into the open. Two inches of snow accumulated during the early morning hours. A smile creased her lips when she discovered pristine snow, no tracks. Nature quietly froze her breath with the gently falling flakes. People sealed their homes from winter. Streams of smoke channeled paths to the heavens.

Upon reaching Gorlovka, Natasha hiked well populated routes to the quarry. Little cutting would get done on this day. The extreme cold would shatter many new blocks. Workers straggled in. Soon, the elder she visited previously, entered the quarry, casually smoking a pipe.

Recognizing her, he jerked his pipe, "You should not be here. He had urgent medical demands to attend. *Girl, he will find you when he is ready.*" The man searched for informants. Everyone looked familiar. "Return to the same barn."

Blushing for her mistake, she nodded with anticipation and gratitude.

Hungry and seeking warmth, Natasha slipped into a bakery. Built upon a bluff overlooking the Donet River, Gorlovka towered above valleys of golden fields during the spring and summer. She gazed over the valley and dreamt occasionally escaping from scripted calculations. Although hours passed slowly, the owner, about the same age as her father, remained pleasant allowing her to study without interruption. He barely kept pace with the demand for hot, fresh baked breads and pastries. By noon, the snow diminished and the clouds gradually broke. The wind expired with the evening quarry whistle. The student packed her book and retraced her steps to the barn.

Anticipating her grandfather's reception drew images of caution, warning, joy, and ambiguity. She entered the barn humming. Upon closing the door, she felt a blow to her head, then to her stomach doubling her over. Another blow to her back sent her reeling to the floor. Heat trickled along the back of her neck. Instinctively attempting to rise, she caught a blow to her chest. Disoriented, her arm was wrenched sharply behind her back to her shoulder blade. A knee pinned her neck and face into the soil moistened by saliva dripping from her mouth. She gasped for air. An ice cold steel blade pinched her jugular. Her head throbbed in pain. Fine gravel pierced her chin.

"Don't say a word," a voice ordered, "or I'll cut you where you lie!"

She'd heard stories about Russian agents, but now she believed them.

"Listen." He pulled her hair. She struggled to breath. She heard two stealing her air.

"You no longer have the freedom to move, to talk, to leave, to even think . . . You do exactly as you are told."

One cinched a band of cloth over her eyes. Lifting her by her arms, he commanded, "Brush yourself off."

Knowing she was filthy and bloody, she randomly wiped straw away. A rough cloth scratched her cheek as an assailant wiped blood from her nose. Fear numbed the pain.

Stumbling as they dragged her, she was forced, staged to sit on a straw bail.

"We'll be waiting somewhere in the barn. You sit patiently making yourself presentable for your grandfather. We want to hear your conversation. His own testimony will silence him to the bowels of Siberia. Your freedom? Depends on whether you want it or not. At all times, your lives are in jeopardy. Understand?"

She felt the tip of the blade drive a bit further.

"Yes," she choked.

"Count aloud to one hundred and remove the blind . . . Begin."

Shivering, paralyzed in terror, she began to count wincing in pain with each number. She heard them rustling about, throwing objects and bails to distract her senses from locating them.

Finished, silent, she tentatively removed the blind. She felt the back of her head. Tacky, warm blood pasted her fingers. She wiped the inside of her coat failing to clean them. The loft doors hung ajar. A full moon cast a blue hue upon the main level.

Gathering straw to insulate her from the cold, the captive felt pain flush her head and squeeze her ribs. A large door squeaked as it swung open. Petrified, she watched the silhouette of a man enter. With caution, he removed his gloves and stepped into the moonlight.

"Natasha . . ."

"Yes." She whispered fighting tears. The dark figure, short in stature, was not what she had imagined. White hair encircled a balding crown. Muscular forearms tensed. He stood strong and healthy for a man in his late sixties. He stepped close to her. He offered a hand before her. It was warm and scarred much like his face. He leaned to kiss her cheek and embraced her. She stiffened with pain smothering an audible release. He joined her sitting on the bail.

"I apologize for my absence all these years." His apprehensive smile begged acceptance. "What a true blessing it is to receive you on Christmas Eve! I am proud of you. I have heard you are studying engineering in Moscow. And are you working to understand and to apply the principles of engineering science?"

"Yes, I am grandpa."

"Good, good. We need good engineers. If we had responsible construction in Chernobyl, we would not have had that catastrophe." The tone of his voice eased her fear. He chuckled, "You will make grand discoveries to aid our people and perhaps the people of the world." He paused to avoid dominating their first conversation.

"I am troubled, grandpa. Why do you bring our family shame?" She swallowed hard as if she were humble prosecution at trial.

"It is not my intention to bring the family shame," he defended. "I bring truth." He presented his hands skin calloused and cracked. "This mind, these hands are gifts to be shared with those in pain and suffering. I should not be prevented from setting a bone, transplanting a kidney, or removing a tumor, because of a man's beliefs, lack of money, or ethnic association."

"But you condemned the war."

"We don't need the oil of the Persian Gulf. We have plenty of uranium for nuclear power and some of the richest coal fields in the world. Our economy is stimulated by war and the employment it creates. What good is it to be a world power when so many of your people live in poverty, refuse to be self-motivated, and lack so much education that your natural resources are wasted or go unnoticed." He innocently cross-examined. "What makes you so unique, so special, that you get such a beneficial education?"

"I work very hard! I obey the State!"

"There are many more like you who work hard and are denied a basic human right to be educated." Steam rose from his lips. "We are not alone."

She ignored his warning, thirsting for information. "But why Christmas and profess to believe in God? Is it because you can't explain everything through science and you refuse to admit your own inadequacies?"

Leo sighed, studying crystal stars glittering from the majestic heavens. His eyes seemed to glow in the midnight blue eve. He drew a deep breath.

"We generate far more questions than we answer. The more we attempt to escape to order, the more aware we become of the world's evolving chaos. There is a force beyond us, a power unmoved by weapons, and a peace no army can destroy. We must surrender what we are for what we might become."

Innocent excitement poured forth from his eyes, like that of a child bubbling of a new discovery. "Natasha . . . two weeks ago, I performed two identical surgeries for two children. Both were quite serious. The first went well. The second had complications. Knowing the first would live, I spent much time tending to the second. This child was much stronger than me. I was scared and she was calm." Tears welled in his eyes. "She was a tough kid. I prayed many hours . . . She died. Her pain and suffering were over. I do not understand. I witnessed a peace and strength in her, a peace and strength I cannot give. I proclaim renewal of life and hope each year. I affirm the enduring 'hope' the holy family lived on their first journey."

He paused. His sight, adjusted to the darkness, scanned the barn. "Natasha, I know they are here."

Tears blazed her swollen cheeks. As she began to speak, his light touch softened the cuts on her lips.

"I knew before you returned. I hope you are not seriously hurt." He gently touched her tender cheeks. Smiling, he diagnosed. "You'll have a shiner in the morning."

"I have waited many years to hold you. God has delivered you to me. Despite the bitterness you may harbor for me . . ." His eyes begged for nothing more than compassion.

Consumed in his gentle touch, Natasha recognized that her grandfather had sacrificed every freedom and right, his career, to be present with her, someone who would criticize his principles, his practices, his very being. He sacrificed himself to be with her.

Natasha's assailants revealed themselves with guns aimed to destroy. Leo embraced his granddaughter.

As the agents converged, the barnyard doors swung wide. Three figures emerged in the rays of the moon. Deputy Vorotnikov stood in the center.

"Hello, doctor. I have finally found you."

"I've always been here, Deputy." Leo nodded respectfully.

"I am reminded, often. Your benevolent practice precedes you." Motioning to the agents, he commanded, "Put your guns away. Wait outside." They did as instructed.

"Why must you work so hard at bringing such trouble?" The deputy didn't expect an answer. "Why do you give me such headaches and chest pains?" Dmitri inquired, exhaling, attempting to lighten the burden.

"It's the borscht." Leo mimicked a serious tone. They laughed briefly, together.

"You have brought Christmas to Gorlovka and I am ordered to take it away. Now, how do you propose I perform such a task?" He spread his arms genuinely welcoming suggestions.

"You can take me, but you are naïve to believe I am more than Christmas. Christmas is in the hearts of many, many of our people. Besides, if Gorbachev's elections become reality, we may pass each other, you to the quarry and me going home," Leo negotiated. He spoke with confidence and compassion. "You outnumber and beat my defenseless granddaughter when all she did was come to me out of love. She has more life than all of you."

Dmitri turned and walked to the doors.

"Where are you going, Deputy?" Leo asked.

"Home . . ., I am tired. Merry Christmas, comrade Tatyana. Take care of your sick."

He disappeared beyond the doors. Stillness, moonlight embraced them. Natasha stared at her grandfather. He had no gun, no troops, and no foul information, only hope for humanity and overwhelming love for her.

Her whisper interrupted winter's silence. "There is a Spirit in the air."

"Oh yes," he sighed, "a Christmas Spirit originating with an infant's cry, enduring in the hearts of all." He kissed her wrapping an arm around her waist to assist her toward the doors. "Merry Christmas, Natasha, Merry Christmas!"

Merry Christmas © 1989
written by Tim Morrison

Dedicated to those who fight oppression for human rights and social justice.

(1) White, Peter T., "The World of Tolstoy," National Geographic, June 1986, p. 788.

Mystic Wind

Rumors dissolved details of an event erased for eternity. This man has never been significant to any life she has shared nor has any recollection of his history in another's life. He has reentered hers and a family's by the fate of rising from his afternoon nap tucked beneath a large sycamore, only to fire a shot into a flying spirit, extinguishing his freedom.

Damp decaying leaves ushered slugs sliming his forehead as he battled to recover his senses. Intense heat enflamed his pores. Tremors oscillated from his mind's epicenter to its outer realm ricocheting pain to his sinuses. Deafening cries of panic warned of fear and chaos. Witnesses to all action on the forest floor, sycamores outstretched branches severed the heavens into turquoise and shades of violet. Like fiery veins from a volcano, blood trickled across his face, burning his eyes. Gradually, sound diminished, light disappeared and all physical sensation surrendered to darkness . . . silence . . . stillness.

Unlike mysterious life pulsing through nature's forest, technology's sterile environment protected him from external dangers. An antagonizing 'ring' reverberated in his left ear, quenching any stimulus from the left.

"Sam."

The voice he had heard somewhere before sounded distorted, fractured in timbre. Instinctively tilting his head in the direction of the voice, Samuel Birch glimpsed the forlorn eyes of his father. Reflections from his window overlooking the roof of a lower floor, accurately traced the salve and bandages guarding his wounds.

"You're going to be fine, Son. Everything's going to be okay." His father reassured him while his eyes blinked doubt.

The junior cocked his head to channel words clearly. He massaged his ear to unplug it.

"You lost one." There was no tact and Samuel appreciated that. Mr. Birch tapped him on the shoulder. "You'll adjust. You'll bounce back."

His elder, sitting in a chair beside the bed, questioned. "Do you remember what happened?"

"I . . . I . . ." Samuel stuttered, paranoid his voice may have been taken, also. "I remember a loud blast." The words resonated in a dead cavity. "The next thing I knew, I was staring into the sky, clouds collapsing into each other. I thought I was gonna die."

Tears smeared into reality the phenomenon of death at sixteen.

Hearing Samuel's revelation, his father sought to comfort him.

Casting brilliant rays, the sun evaporated depression's hostile attack. Paralyzed at his bedroom window, Samuel watched the Sheriff's sedan roll over the gravel drive. Rudely interrupting, the television announcer recapped a grand highlight of the Volunteers-Crimson Tide post-Thanksgiving Day game.

"Sheriff Jesse's here!" His mother proclaimed.

As Sam entered the living room, the temperate sheriff exchanged greetings with the teen's parents. Conscious of his facial deformation, Sam selected a chair against the window exposing his unblemished right side.

Hardened by fighting years of deception and abuse, Sheriff Jesse remained a compassionate, judicious woman. Maturing in Gainesboro, she recognized residents by name in the small Smokey Mountain community of forty-five hundred. Lumber mills populated lowland forests. Created female and elected into law enforcement elevated her image among citizens living in the region. Her profound integrity for justice earned respect.

"You're healing quickly, Sam, considering your unfortunate accident, one, I regret occurred," she complimented attempting to establish a receptive climate.

Mrs. Birch offered to ease any awkwardness. "Would you care for some coffee or something to drink?"

"No thank you. I don't want to wear out my welcome." Sheriff Jesse smiled. Redirecting her attention, she recited, "I was told you don't remember anything about the incident except the blast." She paused expecting a response.

"I remember jogging through the woods and a blast from nowhere and that's it." He repeated what he had been told. "Dad told me old man Jeremiah Jackson pumped me full of buckshot *while hunting.*" Sam's inflection purposely challenged *accident* from her earlier compliment.

"As near as I have been able to recreate the incident, that is correct." Direct eye contact and poise issued confidence in her investigation.

She paused to consider her delivery of the sequence of events for which the Birch family would not be receptive.

"Mr. Jackson delivered you to St. Joseph's Hospital. According to him, he was hunting quail on the edge of a clearing. Exhausted, he relaxed against a tree and dozed. Startled by his dog who inadvertently stirred a pair of birds into the air, Mr. Jackson, reacting on instinct, revolved and fired in the birds' direction. He did not anticipate you entering his firing range at extremely close distance. As you mentioned, you had no idea Mr. Jackson was in the woods. Because you were in a state of shock and unconscious, he carried you through the woods to his truck."

Sheriff Jesse guarded against trivializing Sam's injuries. She desired balance in clarifying them as not life threatening.

For a moment, Mr. Birch tried to imply intent to Mr. Jackson's action.

"I think Sam would have been aware if quail had gone to flight right before he was shot if that, indeed, did happen."

In an effort to deflect another scenario, she countered, "Some might draw the same conclusion, inferring incorrectly, that Mr. Jackson was defending his property from trespassers. No dead birds were found at the scene. As near as I could determine that was the only shot fired. However, there are lots of hunters in forest and any number of them could have been involved, but . . . Jeremiah immediately took full responsibility for what he had done."

". . . And about my son's hearing? What are you going to do about that?" A father's dissension advocated punishment.

Absorbing the season's remnants of burnt oranges and reds, Jesse pondered the questions. Through the plate glass, her gaze searched the mysterious haze drifting through the peaks. Her empathy would fail to revive hearing. She knew no answer would satisfy the real estate broker, and yet a diplomatic answer was the key to securing time for her investigation to establish truth and clear the path for *healing.*

As if reading Braille embossed in oak, she slid her fingertips across the chair rail before her. She drew her summation. "The man has nothing to heal your son's loss."

Mr. Birch's frown demanded revenge for equity in loss.

"All he has," Jesse accounted without defending the man, "is a little worthless acreage which can't be developed, a dog, a shack . . . and a gun."

Mr. Birch fired, "Surely, you've taken that away, haven't you?" insinuating utmost ignorance if she had not.

"No, I haven't."

Sam's mother sighed with frustration, but before she could interject the sheriff continued.

"Jeremiah has lived out east of town for six decades. He's basically a hermit. He draws no welfare from the state. He's always been self-sufficient. He's an excellent marksman, using a firearm only while hunting."

As impersonal as it was about to sound, she hastened for closure. "I regret Sam's tragedy. I have staked Mr. Jackson's property with trespassing signs."

Rising, Mr. Birch approached their executor of the law. Neck muscles stained over a bulging pulse. Lips pursed tightly. A dog on a leash, he restrained his temper.

"This is what I want." He listed demands. "I want his land. I want his gun. And I want him committed to some institution." He pulled the oak wheel from beneath her hands. "Do I make myself clear?" He finished rhetorically, expecting to win the moment's struggle with eye contact.

"You want everything in a tidy package, including a man's life to go with it." Though he encroached, she maintained her composure. Recollections of her childhood interrupted the continuity of her thoughts. She had captured baby bunnies around Jeremiah's pond, snuck up and launched eggs onto the roof of his shanty, perpetuated horror stories of witches and evil haunting the old man and his grounds and, yet . . . he never retaliated. To her, he was a hermit. His name occupied an infinitesimally small place in her memory for over forty years. Rumors dissolved details of an event erased for eternity.

This man had never been significant to any life she shared nor had she any recollection of his history in another's life. He had reentered hers and a family's by the fate of rising from his afternoon nap tucked beneath a large sycamore, only to fire a shot into a flying spirit, extinguishing his freedom. She empathized with Sam's loss, but she refused to abandon Jeremiah's defense.

"It will take some time . . ." She paused and walked to the door to let herself out. "What you have demanded, you will undoubtedly get. Jeremiah won't fight you and the evidence is, without question, in your favor."

Sheriff Jesse assumed her exit through the doorway as her entrance into nature, a space others were not allowed to encroach. She glanced over her shoulder. "I'll keep in touch." She returned to anonymity behind her tinted lenses.

Sunshine burned the dense fog cloaking the valleys and crevices of the Great Smokey Mountains. Rolling hills sparkled with diamonds of melting morning frost. Birds praised the day's glorious sun, feeding and basking in the sun's radiant shower.

Samuel dreaded the feeding frenzy of gossip among three hundred students at Timberline High. Those who'd heard the embellished stories anticipated witnessing the carnage.

The throbbing pain dramatically diminished. His lack of hearing depressed his mental state. Carefully, he applied the ointments, treating the cuts and abrasions. Medications moistened the wounds to prevent cracking, when the skin stretched while speaking or reacting with emotion.

Crowding the average in several classes, he knew negotiating an excused absence with his father was futile. His mother's sympathy was easy prey. However, the consequences of a devious victory might weigh heavily against his margin.

Slipping into his coat, he grabbed his lunch and hoisted his book bag over his shoulder. As he stepped onto the porch, he nearly tripped over a basket filled with assorted fruits. He quickly swung it up onto the kitchen counter.

"Where'd that come from?" His mother smiled with childlike expectations.

He shrugged. "I found it next to the front door." He removed a pear and an apple to reveal a rough leather scrap with a crude imprint of what appeared to be the letter 'J'.

Frowning, Sam massaged the leather with his fingers as if to erase the imprint. "It's either a bad joke or it's from that old man."

"Your father won't accept this. Looks like the old man's offering fruit to salvage his junk yard." Her tone echoed vengeance.

As predicted, Sam recalled the scent of decaying leaves as he dispelled rumors concerning the shooting. Students inflated tales of trespassing onto the old man's grounds on occasions of dares that the place was haunted.

Sound aggravated him most. It resonated in his head due to the pressure building behind the clotted blood. Doctors had explained that after the ear had healed to a certain point, the clot could be removed and the pressure permanently relieved. Subconsciously, he naturally cocked his receptive ear toward the speaker, compromising eye contact. Occasionally, he consciously acted to correct his equilibrium, maintaining a straight path along hallways, in and out of classrooms. Losing tone quality as he manipulated the strings of his guitar pushed him toward depression. His compositions lacked apparent pitch and harmonics for which he had grown accustomed.

The sun dipped below the horizon splashing brilliant reds and oranges across the sky. Samuel pumped himself with optimism as he walked home. Doctors promised each day to be better than the day before. Eventually, time would mend his wounds as he developed new perspectives to sound and music.

Twice each week, fruit baskets mysteriously appeared on the driveway or lawn with a small woodcarving or leather letter imprinted with a 'J'. No one ever saw Jeremiah come or go. Once Samuel sat watching from the darkness of his living room. Pausing for buttered popcorn, he returned to discover a basket nestled to the front door.

Monday, during the week of Christmas, Samuel retrieved another gift of fruit. No impression was found. Beneath some oranges, he uncovered a medallion.

"Let me see that," Mr. Birch requested. Examining the tarnished metal, he bellowed, "The old man's giving it his last gasp . . . thinking I won't complete the papers. I'll own everything he has by Wednesday!"

He gave the tarnished, but well-crafted medal to his son. "You'd better get to school before you're late."

Unassuming, Samuel slid the medal into his pocket. Privately, he pulled it forth several times to study its constitution. At day's end, he returned to Mr. Weisman's history class. As the historian scrutinized essays he collected earlier, Samuel entered, wishing to interrupt, yet apprehensive to do so.

"Samuel!" his mentor exclaimed. "What burst of brilliance brings you to his hallowed place of decades past?"

Mr. Weisman had a peculiar way of making the mundane intriguing. Fanatical about the Civil War Era, his eyes gleamed with excitement . . . and the intriguing stories he told were worth a price of admission.

Shuffling the papers before him, he quickly set them aside to give Samuel his undivided attention.

His student choked, suppressing his voice as if he had stolen the medallion. "I need some information." Revealing the piece, he gently displayed the decoration on the desk. He stared into his elder's eyes expecting an explanation.

Mr. Weisman's expression and delicate handling enhanced the value of the unknown. Opening the left hand drawer, he pulled forth a bottle of Listerine, rinsed his mouth, and gulped a swallow. Grimacing, he gasped.

Carefully pressing the wrinkled blue silk ribbon, as not to damage a single thread, he cross examined, "Ah . . . Son, this is no ordinary medal. Where'd you get this?"

"I received it in a fruit basket on my driveway."

Peering with disbelief, Weisman wary of his student's skepticism, "With this medallion in hand, I wouldn't tell anyone either!" He held it in his fingers as if cradling a baby bird.

"This is the Medal of Honor. The white stars embroidered into the blue ribbon represent the original thirteen states of the Union." A golden eagle's talons clutched the word 'valor' below the cast silhouette of a soldier's head encompassed by the five points of a large star.

He turned it over in his hand to reveal a crude etching. "'1864,'... The man who received the army's highest distinction, the Congressional Medal of Honor must have fought gallantly with vigor and bravery!"

He went to the drawer for a second shot and rinse.

"Introduced for the first time during the Civil War, this is the most distinguished honor bestowed on any man for a courageous act."

Samuel thought Mr. Weisman was about to break into tears with his emotional delivery.

"Some man sacrificed his existence for the life of another, without question, during a war in which brother fought brother and father fought son."

A glaze shadowed his eyes. Mesmerized by the medal, he stared, whispering. "Sacrificed his life, his very self, for what he might become . . . such courage . . . such faith . . ."

As soon as his mother concluded thanksgiving, his father sliced the roast and served his family. Steamed broccoli and asparagus accented mashed potatoes and thick rich gravy.

"Seems odd, it's Christmas Eve. We haven't received a basket since the one containing . . ." Sam tapered his sense of loss with the abrupt halt.

His father remained indifferent concerning the medal's identity and essence. Reaching for a manila folder, he revealed legal documents along with a land title. He set them before his son. "The old man's not there anymore. Yesterday was supposed to be his final day," his father informed Sam as if he should have known.

Samuel studied the land title. Survey points indicated boundaries. His eyes isolated the striking 'J' scribbled at the bottom of the deed.

Distracted, Sam heard his father add, "He didn't argue or put up a fight. According to Sheriff Jesse, he signed willingly . . ." His father rambled on, but Samuel became so immersed in the significance of the documents, he abandoned the moment.

The heavens shattered as billowing clouds drifted apart, exposing their silhouettes against the moon's powder blue rays.

Samuel's heart thrust from his chest as he scrutinized the path before him. Expecting it to be black and eerie, he was infected with increasing fear and tension as he proceeded.

The stillness and the mystery of the Eve welcomed his steps in the four-inch snow. A single set of tracks trailed while a white slate of destiny awaited him. Synchronized, dark frozen branches cut a jagged sky with glowing ivory lances. Periodically, ice shifted and cracked over the shallow stream snaking parallel to the trail.

Listening to his shallow breaths amidst the moon's brightness, he experienced the deafening silence of nature's invitation to peace and tranquility, where all rested in gentle harmony. Always aware, glancing from one side to another, he felt a presence watching him. With each step forward, an envelope of darkness sealed behind him. Time accompanied him through the forest, eventually reaching his destination.

Some short paces away, a glimmer of flames through a window flickered in what appeared to be the ruins of a wilderness check station.

Suddenly, the serenity of the forest was carved from his heart with the wicked snarl of darkness's beast. Paralyzed with fear, Samuel twisted in the snow to confront his challenger. No position of compromise existed. He trespassed to become the enemy.

Baring his eyeteeth and spitting saliva, offspring from hounds bred with coyotes, glared with vicious malice. Unaware he had been retreating in the snow the intruder had backed into a large oak. Losing his footing on the rising roots, he gathered himself preparing to fight, as flight ceased to be a viable option.

Snapping at his ankles, the animal prepared to engage issuing guttural warnings for attack.

Swifter than the attack might have occurred, an old man erased the line of division between man and beast.

The man abruptly called, but did not shout. "Jake."

Snarling for a moment, the mixed breed backed away, sustaining eye contact with his prisoner.

Trembling with fear and gratitude, Sam lipped some words, but failed to speak. He was unable to identify the man for shadows cast by trees.

The stranger directed him to the log cabin's entrance. "Come in."

Sam's heart choked, feeling it was about to tumble from his chest. Like a sentry Jake escorted them inside.

Heat engulfed the boy's rigid frame. His emerald eyes adjusted to the fireplace. As he scanned the walls of the room, he observed a tanned deer hide draped over horizontal posts and a pair of red fox furs stretched between racks.

Adjusting a chair, lashed together from willow and cottonwood, the boy shuffled close to the amber coals. Intense heat massaged his face. Peering beyond his extended fingers, he noticed the dirt floor below. Twisting the toe of his shoe into the hard packed surface, he scraped a dusty layer of soil. To confirm, he bent to touch it.

Although primitive, Jeremiah's quarters offered peace. Warmer, Samuel slid lower into his chair and studied the log rafters overhead. Shadows, like knights, jousted among the triangular designed tresses. Chaotic patterns courted Samuel's images and understanding of the last month's events. So many spoke of a man named Jeremiah. But no one 'knew' the man. No one informed Sam . . . Jeremiah was a Chickasaw.

As if interpreting some vision, his host stared into the fiery blue flames ravaging the wood. Smooth creases defined his weary chestnut eyes and high cheekbones. Fairly youthful in appearance, he did not appear hard or aged, as compared to pictures the student associated with Sitting Bull or Crazy Horse. Dark braids wrapped behind his neck, tucked into a tight weave. Muscular and average in size, Jeremiah seemed in a trance. One clasped over another, his hands were scarred and firm. A golden glow gently caressed and lightened his dark complexion.

Abandoning his preconceived notions of a Civil War hero from the North, perhaps Indiana, Ohio, or Pennsylvania, Sam glanced behind Jake relaxed, lying between them. A large stuffed military duffel leaned against the wall next to the door.

"You going somewhere . . . ?" shattered the silence. A spike in Sam's pulse poked his heart.

Jeremiah's eyes remained fixed on the crackling logs. "Yes . . ." barely audible.

"Where?"

"The mountains."

Sam envisioned seclusion, snow, and waterfalls frozen over wedged rock formations.

"I didn't expect to find you here, tonight." The intruder uttered believing the opposite.

Jeremiah spoke gently without facing his fireside companion. "I expected you, . . . I prayed to the Great Spirit each night . . . hoping He brings you to me."

"Hoping?"

"Yes . . ."

"I don't understand."

"I . . . I think you do . . . otherwise . . . you would not have come. Fear would have severed your nerve to enter the darkness in the wilderness."

A shiver slithered along his spine.

"I saw what I had done." A tear glistened in the glow from his face. "I have brought shame to my home. The sun is fading on my spirit and when I go, I want to go without shame."

Patiently, the once injured internalized the words. He admitted, "I watched from my room at night for the opportunity to see you, perhaps to speak with you . . ."

A smile creased the Native's lips. "I know."

"You saw me, right?"

"No, I know young boys have much curiosity," he said grinning, "I simply fed it."

"You could have left me that day. The wounds were not life threatening. I never saw you. I could not identify you," he testified.

"For what price? The price my soul, my integrity?"

Digging into his pocket, Samuel presented the medallion. Suspending it from the ribbon, he laid the medal respectfully into his palm. "Whose was this?"

Jeremiah recognized the decoration with fond memories. "It was my grandfather's. He was a Chickasaw scout for the Union under General Cruft in Richmond, Kentucky. Generals Manson and Nelson were surrounded and captured behind Confederate battle lines. He led the 16th and 55th Brigades through Confederate strongholds back to Rogersville saving the lives of many men unfamiliar with the territory."

"Very few Chickasaw fought for the Federals. Some had slaves of their own and moved under economic pressure into Oklahoma. My grandfather grew up in Paducah, Kentucky. He heard Lincoln speak. He became an instant believer. At sixteen, he enlisted."

"Shortly after I was born, my father died of pneumonia. My grandfather named me Mystic Wind. He said the Great Spirit would guide me with wisdom. While most of the Chickasaw resettled to the west among the Comanche, he decided to settle this land after the Battle of Chickamauga ravaged it. When he died, he left three gifts his horse, his Medal of Honor, and his pipe."

Mystic Wind reached for a pipe at the base of his chair. He handed it to Samuel. Carvings melded the changing seasons, depicted symbols of fertility and prosperity along the body, the length of his forearm. Leather tassels with artistic bead designs dangling below the mouthpiece and the carved cherry bowl.

"My grandfather could solve any problem. He had great wisdom!" He accepted the ceremonial pipe from his guest. "When my grandfather died, I took this medal and pipe. I rode his horse to the bluff overlooking the Cumberland River. Angry, I tossed the medal over the edge. Each brave created his own pipe. I embraced his close to my heart . . . I was fifteen . . ." Mystic Wind packed the pipe with tobacco he had grown.

"When I am in the company of man, I feel frustrated and out of control. Although I do not understand it, when I am with nature, I feel His presence. Immediately, I climbed down the bluff to search for the medal. I was amazed how quickly I found it. It was then that I trusted the Spirit was with me."

The flames hypnotized the Chickasaw. The medal's value inherent with the Spirit returned a young brave's grandfather during the torment of death and separation. Samuel understood the agony Mystic Wind experienced as a consequence of the accident before Thanksgiving.

Unfolding the legal documents entitling his father to Jeremiah's land, Sam tossed them into the flames. They blanketed the glowing coals at their feet. Together, both watched the white parchment brown, and then burst into flames setting their faces aglow.

Tears formed in the Chickasaw's eyes as Samuel pinned the Medal of Honor to his elder's flannel shirt. Lighting the pipe, Jeremiah passed it to his brother. Sam inhaled once and offered it whispering, "May the Great Spirit of Christmas erase all shame and bring you peace."

Merry Christmas © 1992
written by Tim Morrison

Dedicated to those who are working to recover from mistakes they think are too great to be forgiven.

Christmas Predicaments

Illness forced him to renounce his pride and to seek peace with his family cut at its base to search for fortune and rank.

"I'll get it!" Alex yelled as she raced to the front door anticipating Shari's arrival.

She opened the door to discover an older gentleman dressed for woodworking in a red plaid flannel shirt and cotton pants. His eyes expressed as much surprise to see the seventeen-year-old youth as she expressed disappointment in her best friend's punctuality. Alexis appeared so much more mature and energetic than he had imagined from the periodic photos he received. It was apparent she did not recognize him. Gus thought it best not to introduce himself without her mother's consent.

"Is your mother home?" he inquired, refraining from the natural tendency to introduce oneself to a stranger.

"Just a moment." Absorbed in her plans, Alex disappeared into the living room and called. "Mom, it's for you."

Whisking the soil from her fingers, Samantha set the repotted plant aside and rinsed her hands. As she intersected Alex rushing upstairs, Sam attempted to capture a glimpse of a guest her daughter was unlikely to know. Easing the door wider, Sam froze, paralyzed with confusion.

"Dad, what in the world brings you here?" Over twelve years elapsed since Samantha heard her father's threats.

Bitter arguments regarding her marriage to Martin severed ties between father and daughter. As an environmentalist, Martin's support stringent regulations on logging and for the preservation of virgin forest fueled antagonism with Gus, the spokesman for commercial lumbermen and, unfortunately, Samantha's father.

Elected negotiator for the lumbermen's association, Gus Buchner was recognized as an intelligent, savvy strategist. His knowledge and experience in forestry formed his platform on responsible lumbering. However, economic pressures and fanatical environmentalism propelled his aging temper. Unemployment and inflation dismantled lumber milling communities, fragmenting families and eroding incomes. Adversaries evolved as the workforce he represented were later forced to lay off. Surviving numerous labor disputes, Gus retired having weathered the onslaught of abuse and accusations from many who felt he surrendered too easily, cowered to liberals, and secretly favored his son-in-law's sentiments. In truth, Gus despised Martin for innocently weaving his relationship to his daughter with his environmental convictions. Gus refused to relinquish the fight. Unfortunately, his relationship to his daughter fell among the spoils, surrendering her in marriage to an adversary. He pushed her away pressing her with his bitterness, anger, and pride.

Frequently concealing his position, Gus seldom spoke first. He conceded, "I'm here in peace, no lumberjacks . . . I'm pretty sick, Sam . . . I have come here to die. I don't want to die alone." Pride precluded further revealing his fears.

Emotions saturated her thoughts strangling any response. Guilt invaded, percolating memories. She contemplated the extreme circumstances at work in her father to humble himself. Fortunately, at that instant, her anxious teen thundered down the stairs shattering the tension, mumbling something about Shari driving them to Logger's Park for an afternoon cookout. Buffering his distance, Gus trailed his excited granddaughter out onto the Victorian porch. Samantha followed. Neither spoke as she climbed into the GMC with her friend. The vehicle quickly disappeared over cracking gravel.

Brilliant orange, yellow, and red leaves fluttered from towering sycamores, reflecting sunlight as fall breezes swept them across the lawn.

"Kind of prophetic, don't you think? I imagine you predicted it would take something this serious to bring us together." He murmured stepping across the painted floorboards.

Samantha's eyes traced his movement as she listened.

"I have pancreatic cancer."

Somehow inappropriately out of sequence, her mind struggled to validate his admission.

"Why?"

"Hell, I don't know why," he cranked attempting to shadow his predicament. "God knows it wasn't my idea!"

"I'm scared. I don't want to die. I don't want to be alone." He leaned against one of the pillars.

"I'm confused." Fighting insensitivity, she continued, "You cast us out of your life years ago. We're all scared. Why us?"

Although he realized he might have erred in judgment, Gus refused to admit fault or guilt. His ocean blue eye captured hers. "I don't know my granddaughter. You're supposed to understand your kids, but I don't understand you. I have too many questions and too little time to answer them. I'm out of control and I'll never be in control again."

"You've been out of control for a long time, Dad."

Gus repressed the instantaneous joy surging within as he heard the recognition, 'Dad'!

Samantha sat on the porch rail allowing the cool breeze to wash the heat away during this awkward moment. She ran her fingers through her chestnut curls.

"You despise Martin and now you want to live under his roof?"

"It's not ideal," he admitted, eyes darting away searching for a compromise. "I'll stay in my room out of harm's way until you call."

"I genuinely want to help, but you've said some really nasty, threatening things. I suspect you may attempt to drive a wedge between Martin and me, which is ultimately unfair to Alex. I will not allow you to disrupt our lives while manipulating our sympathies."

"I have no such intention. I confess," he offered before she could interrupt, "after you were married I had plenty of intention. Who knows? Maybe I can do something . . . for you, for Alexis . . . maybe even for Martin."

"It took years for me to reconcile the bitterness I felt when you didn't even show at our wedding."

"But I did visit the hospital after Alexis' birth."

"And . . .," she refuted, "you antagonized Martin about policy and legislation while he should have been celebrating her birth." Squinting, Samantha grinned. "I was especially annoyed when you argued with Martin while at the same time you shielded yourself with Alexis cradled in your arms."

"Actions of a good strategist," he embraced her smile with his.

The colorful patchwork of leaves shifted with the breeze. Both knew further immediate mental acrobatics would never heal wounds suffered from the previous twelve years. Life presented yet another predicament for which the solution lies within the process of living.

Samantha retrieved a small twig lying on the deck and snapped it in two. "You may stay in the bedroom across the hall from Alexis. I'll post a ladder outside your window for you to come and go without interference." She extended one small stick. "This is as close to an olive branch as I can get."

Gus reached for it without touching it. "And bathroom privileges?" he bantered clutching the stick.

"Once after dawn and again before midnight, she offered with a hint of apprehension.

Awkwardly displaying gratitude, he smiled, resigning eye contact. Sam felt strength and confidence as she released the twig to her father. Of two thoughts, one to embrace him out of familial empathy and the other to accept his unspoken request to reconcile and resurrect a relationship they buried years ago, only the second prevailed.

After selecting a young physician opening his practice in the small Oregon community, Gus positioned pictures, though dated, at his desk and dresser. As if it was fragile, he carefully inserted his granddaughter's senior picture into the corner of a frame circling a smiling five year old. *What was so important that I missed so much of your life?* His fingertips touched glass seeking to read her face. He slid a box of intimate letters he'd collected from Samantha and friends next to a recliner. He remained secluded to avoid disrupting the family routine.

Alexis, always gregarious, shared stories of friends and activities while managing her social schedule. At home, her music wrapped her in privacy. Often she dined while dashing to rehearsals with the high school jazz ensemble. Burning the midnight oil to avoid sensitive conversations with his father-in-law, Martin composed initiatives for environmental legislation. Surprising to Gus, Martin's professional aggressiveness diminished to a quiet passion at home. Frequently, Samantha and her father weaved stories reconstructing their lives from the special events they'd missed during their separation.

Philip, a home care specialist, was appointed to care for Gus for the duration of his illness. Samantha insisted the entire family be present for Philip's instructions on hospice care. He spoke with precision reading expressions for understanding. Philip's fluent gestures effused kindness. Daily, he witnessed the pain and suffering of death, the loss of precious loved ones. With each, mystery transcended the closing chapter of this life to open another. Experiencing one's death carried no guarantee of revelation with it.

As the black French Canadian outlined a machine positioned on an oak bookcase against the wall, he tapped the top. "This is a PAC-Patient Controlled Analgesic machine. Miniature pumps and vacuums regulate the medication prescribed to subdue the pain. If you recall, we threaded a pic line, peripheral intravenous catheter, into a space beneath your shoulder to the subclavian vein, which runs to your heart. Heparin keeps blood from clotting in the line after a drawn dosage."

He stretched a small transparent tube and directed his attention to Gus. "This runs from the PAC to your catheter. I recommend you change this tubing every three days or so because bacteria may develop and spread in the line."

His gentle smile draped those stressed with comfort and courage. "I encourage you to exercise, get outside, enjoy nature. Only use PAC when the pain is frequent or overbearing. When you feel the need, relax in the recliner. Insert the tube into the catheter and push this button for your medication. Your pain threshold determines the frequency of medication. If you have any questions or complications, my number is posted on the side of the machine." Philip explained his 'checkups' would gradually increase in frequency after a couple months.

Philip graciously answered questions with sensitivity. He explained emergency protocol. Martin observed every detail, fearing Samantha was too consumed reconciling her past and Alexis was too absorbed in senior activities. Gus felt mortality squeezing him.

Light sliced through a gap in the bedroom door leading to her grandfather. Hesitating, Alexis tapped on the door.

"Yes."

She slowly entered to find him relaxing in his chair. Dim light cast vague shadows upon the walls. A faint golden hue illuminated the room. A cool breeze chilled it. A brilliant flash cut a jagged path across the black September sky. Moments later, thunder rattled the Victorian panes. Droplets slithered down the glass and rhythmically trickled onto the sill.

Alexis eased herself onto the corner of the bed. Tentative, Gus didn't appear to be in need of the solace she planned to extend. Although she felt immune to death, exchanging her thoughts intimidated her. Her grandfather's cancer heightened the urgency she felt to build their relationship.

Initially, he felt awkward. Ordinarily, Gus wouldn't have had the time or the patience to share conversation with a teen. However, he anticipated her enthusiasm and welcomed her visit.

"We have too many rainy days and Monday's," she sighed issuing subtle humor. "Rain's depressing after a while."

He watched the wind wave through the cottonwoods. "I like storms . . . kind of nature's percussion."

The gentle breeze lifted her melancholy. Silence made her nervous. "Aren't you cold?"

"Not really, I was somewhere else . . . Rain eases my mind. The wind and lightning and thunder display . . . such grace and power."

"Where were you before I interrupted?" She invited attempting to lift his spirits.

"One of my favorite childhood places." A mischievous grin curled his lips. "We used to skinny dip there when I was your age."

"Gus, with girls?" She felt herself blush despite having heard more explicit conversations over lunch with friends.

Raising his eyebrows, he chuckled, "The bathing beauties' receptions to our invitations were icier than the water."

"Right," she chided as lightning ignited a spark in her eyes. Seconds later thunder rattled the room.

Alexis listened to the storm momentarily before breaking the silence. "I hope you like it here. If you want to get out, do some runnin' around . . . ?" She stood straightening her robe.

"Runnin' around?" He nodded grinning.

Pleased that she piqued his curiosity, she smiled.

"I want to live life in the time I have remaining rather than try to compensate for my arrogance of the last seventeen years." Cupping his hands offering a gift, he formed his words. "I want to share a small portion of your life, which until now, I've so selfishly pissed away."

"Oh Grandpa, then why are you sitting here?"

The desire to freeze the moment escaped him as she recognized him. *Grandpa* touched his soul. "Because, I'm listening for the first time in a long time. I hear my restlessness, my resentment in the storm . . . And I feel calming in the rain."

She laughed feeling she had nothing to bring him peace. "I think you need a dose of fun." She gracefully stepped to the doorway and whispered, "Good night."

Dense fog lifted and burned in the morning sun. Snow buried the peaks towering above the timberline. Steam rose from the asphalt roadway that spiraling indefinitely into billowing clouds. Alexis wound her four-wheel drive Jeep onto an abandoned logging route as Gus instructed. Rounding an abutment, she downshifted along the descent.

"You must have forgotten the direction." The Jeep idled on the thawing gravel road.

Frustration muted him. "How long's it been like this?"

"Don't know. Usually fallen timbers blockade driving logging roads," she plainly stated.

Alexis could not imagine it like her grandfather described. Brilliant sunlight pierced the murky lake. This was a place he'd once shared with Sam when she was a child. Stumps protruded among a hillside of chestnut, fir, and hemlock seedlings for as far as he could see. Sparse survivors were spared for further growth. The sea of green averaged four feet depth. Erosion reduced the entering stream from roaring white water to a frothy rampage, smearing silt swirls in the jade colored lake. Under pressure for construction and economic development, the wonderland Gus protected as a forest manager for so many years had been harvested after his promotion to Seattle. Ashamed, he felt responsible for its destruction.

Carefully, she backed the Jeep along the sloppy, washboard trail to a fork. Navigating along another gravel trail, she maneuvered farther into the Umpqua Forest into protected, virgin wilderness. The late October snow at the lower elevations melted leaving the forest floor damp and boggy. Towering pines encircled an oval meadow protected by snowcapped Mount Theilsen. The placid lake's surface mirrored century-old oaks and white washed aspens. Earthen tones blended with ashen peaks against the sky's royal blue canvass. Snow at higher elevations glistened with a melting sheen.

They traversed slippery rocks circling the base of a roaring falls to a moist slab baking in sunlight. Enormous natural ice arches extended several feet from crevices cut through the rock high above the lake. Trickles cascaded over jagged edges, riveting into the pool below. Spherical droplets tapped a syncopated rhythm inducing tranquility.

Sparkles danced like fireflies in the elder's eyes mesmerized by the expanding ripples. He admired the fantastic frozen arch sculpted with icicle daggers jutting out over the pool. Tones echoed from hollows formed with centuries of turbulent water. Alexis felt her grandfather's solace and disappointed with the destruction of a tangible piece of his past that he hoped to share. Swimming in cold crystal clear waters, inhaling the aroma of wildflowers and pines, and anxiously awaiting an elk, moose, or an elusive bobcat to grace the afternoon faded to memories. Even the echoes of playful laughter, squeals, and screams were difficult to recall. Illness forced him to renounce his pride and to seek peace with his family cut at its base to search for fortune and rank.

He felt immobilized between supporting survival economics and habitat preservation. With wisdom, Gus recognized how growing global populations stressed natural resources. No easy solutions existed. In reality, those accelerating under capitalistic greed doomed both business and nature. All will suffer severe consequences if extreme action is taken.

"I don't mind if you adopt this site, Gus," Alex whispered, interrupting his thoughts.

"I spent some time protecting lakes such as this, but too little time diving into them," he sighed. Thick thunderheads veiled the peaks encroaching on his time in the forest. He tempted fate, knowing a solid snowstorm at this time of year could easily seal the pass they traveled until early April. He also realized he may never experience such grandeur again.

Compassionately, Alexis asked, "Are you scared, Grandpa?"

"I used to be, but I think I'm past that stage." He joked. "You know psychologists; they're always dividing life into stages. I wish I wasn't in this position." He paused thoughtfully. ". . . I'm in the reconciliation stage."

"I'm trying to reconcile whether I believe I deserve something after this life. I can't imagine what it might be. I do know, I don't want any hand in its design. Sitting here with you leaves little doubt in my mind. Billions of years of patience and care created this jewel. In the not-so-distant future, I hope there is some Creator to thank for such magnificence."

Genuinely surprised, Alexis gave little credence to a Creator, but now was not the time to initiate theological debates.

"Ironically, as much as the loss of my favorite place aggravates me, the slightest glimmer of the past reminds me of so much I've taken for granted."

He changed his tone interjecting a burst of enthusiasm. "Because I was bitter, I abandoned a relationship with your mother. Fortunately, she invited me to stay." Alexis appeared confused. "You and the splendor of the falls fill me with hope."

"What about me?" Alex leaned playfully into his side.

He winked, chuckling, "I'm leaving my ashes to you!"

"Gus!" she exclaimed, thinking the idea preposterous.

"And . . .," he tapped her for emphasis and sincerity, "my travel journals. Many of the northwest natives believe once you've visited a place, a bit of your spirit resides there."

He hid the tear in his eye. "Your time with me is limited. However, my steps are many around the wilderness. I want you to sprinkle a few of my ashes at every place you retrace.

Take a moment to touch and be touched . . . and know I am present."

"This reconciliation stuff is strange. I hope your directions are clear."

"It's an awesome responsibility. I thought it might help to know me. Whatever you do, don't bury me. I don't do mines or caverns."

"I'll sprinkle them everywhere, Grandpa. And I'll sprinkle the most right here!" She kissed his cheek with a promise.

He wanted to embrace her, but felt uncomfortable initiating it. His heart swelled when she wedged her hand between his palms. He clutched it tightly.

Weeks passed. Winter's sinking temperatures closely paralleled the forest manager's declining health. Fighting the relentless desire to inject pain killing morphine, Gus finally succumbed, admitting loss in battle. An hour of sleep in the afternoon multiplied to several each day. Samantha and Martin moved his bed downstairs into the living room adjacent to the PAC. Occasionally, he would murmur gibberish especially after a morphine dose. Nausea wrenched his stomach. Losing weight sucked his skin to his ribs and hollowed his face.

Steady, increasing pain indicated the cancer's proliferation. Greater morphine doses distorted Gus's perspectives of the world. As Thanksgiving arrived, one seat at the festive table remained vacant. Samantha hoped the pain would subside long enough for Gus to savor some delicious turkey vegetable soup. She longed to hear more about his travels and the people he'd met to fill in the voids that existed for so many years in her family history. Instead, she offered thanks for his presence in her life and prayed for relief in his suffering.

After clearing the table, Samantha curled into a large recliner beneath a soft light in the living room. As Gus slept in bed, she allowed her mind to wander into childhood. She smiled, recalling the satisfaction in her father's face as he carried her bright red Schwinn up the basement stairs. The preceding morning she had heard the occasional ping as a wrench hit the concrete floor. Grease and oil stained his fingers.

Engrossed with her birthday bike, Sam almost felt the seat as she mounted the bike while Gus stabilized it from behind. One trial after another, he walked beside her holding the frame as she pedaled, learning to adjust her equilibrium.

Soon, he was running beside her to catch her when she'd wobble. Consumed with the thrill of riding, she gained speed. Suddenly aware of passing trees, she began to waver. Prepared to bale in fear, she glanced over her shoulder to see her father watching from a distance. She had outrun him. He'd let go. Little did Sam understand, she took her initial strides toward independence, a precursor to the future.

Her mind's eye faded as Gus began to stir. His glazed eyes stared through her as if she and this place were foreign to him. Squinting, he gradually steadied himself into a seated position. The daze seemed to lift with his posture.

"Gus . . . are you okay?" Sam ran her fingers through his hair.

He didn't answer. Pointing to his coat hanging on the wall, he stuttered, "I want . . . want . . . to go outside."

Philip's strict instructions fired from memory. "Bundle warmly, overdo it. As the immune system deteriorates, pneumonia lingers as an ever present threat."

As he sat incoherently mumbling instructions, Samantha slid oversized wool socks over his feet, followed by insulated hiking boots. She smiled imagining him doing the same for her when she was a little girl anxiously waiting to romp in the snow.

He lifted his arms like a child as she slid a sweatshirt over his flannel. After wrapping a scarf around his neck, she zipped his coat and topped his head with his favorite multicolored stocking cap with the yarn ball bobbing on top. She assisted him out onto the porch.

In places, the snow was two feet deep. Twice earlier, Martin had shoveled a narrow crevice through the snow the length of their drive and around the house. Interlocking arms, Sam braced her father from slipping down the porch steps. He nearly disappeared in the narrow clearing. The crisp, cold air refreshed his mind, invigorating his spirit. Gus remained silent as she carefully escorted him on the return climb.

Winded, he paused as he'd done on while climbing so many summits in life. "Somebody cut a hell of a gorge. This was a ball buster!" His pride on this trek complimented Martin's labor, liberating him briefly from cancer's entrapment.

He scrutinized the neighborhood turning east then west. "It's a cold son of a buck, but I'll take it!"

Samantha laughed, "I'll take it, too!" Fully appreciating the moment, she banished thoughts of numbered days.

He struggled to breath, but demanded, "I want to go work in Martin's shop."

His request baffled her. They had lapped the house several times in the past, but Martin's private domain, his refuge, naturally seemed to be off limits. Samantha perceived this as a direct assault on hallowed ground.

Gus started slowly toward the small shop. Frozen tree limbs clapped with the wind inspiring his march. Though cold inside, the walls sheltered them from the breeze. Organized by class, tools hung ready for use.

Both hesitated, fascinated by a classic composition centered on a horizontal maple table. Trembling, the forester pulled one glove off and gently touched the glistening wood.

"It's beautiful," he gasped.

"It looks like a vase," Samantha guessed, just as impressed with the craftsmanship as her father.

"It's an urn." Gus stated firmly. Reality silently invaded. He acknowledged the exquisite quality. "The wide, vertical light colored wood is ash. It has a very tight grain. The dark wood between each stave is walnut. The neck and base are cherry."

He carefully tipped the urn to discover a blank brass plate fastened to the bottom. Sam admired Gus' knowledge of wood and admiration of her husband's artistic creativity.

"It's the finest piece I have ever seen," Gus complimented, feeling a gentleness he'd never experienced.

After completing the return trek to the living room, Gus reclined to his pillow, exhausted. Samantha sat in her glider beside him protecting time to simply enjoy his presence as she did frequently nestling Alexis as an infant.

He whispered, "Martin has been a worthy opponent. He is a very good man. I fear I have misjudged him." He closed his eyes to rest.

Sam caressed his gray stubble cheek with her fingers. "Dad, I think Martin's trying to amend the lost time as well." Disappointed, she wasn't sure she had eased Gus' conscience.

Medicated to a delirious state, Gus awoke amidst shouting and confusion.

"Gus, we have an emergency at St. Luke's! Martin's meeting me there!" Samantha deliberately shouted. "We may not come home!" She shook him attempting to break his stupor.

Tears burned her flushed cheeks. Confusion and fear engaged forbidden thoughts.

She continued shouting. "I left a message for Philip to check in on you! He'll be here soon."

Struggling to hold his head up as he leaned against a stuffed cushion, Gus mumbled. "Yeah, go. I know Philip. I may be high, but by gawd I'm not deaf."

The essence behind Sam's tears did not concern him as much as why he thought he might be imagining them.

Strangers just hours earlier, Dr. Pearson, an accomplished yet reserved neurologist in his early fifties, accompanied anxious parents as nurses wheeled Alexis into the intensive care unit, a sterile, technology-driven environment. Garland strung along the hallway heralded the week before Christmas.

With charts tucked beneath his arm, Dr. Pearson detained a heart—broken couple. Their sense of purpose scrambled, both appeared as incoherent as their patient they left behind. Listening for words of hope, their ability to focus fell prey to their imagination.

"Alexis suffered a traumatic head injury. We've identified a fissure in the skull above the forehead where she evidently struck the rear view mirror sending her through the windshield." He illustrated the approximate location with his fingers to his hairline. "We have inserted a shunt inside her head to release fluid pressure." He realized the explanation never sufficed for the witnesses to the consequences. "She is in a coma."

"What's that really mean?" An impassioned father searched for some loophole to negotiate a strategy for saving his daughter's life.

"Her automatic functions such as breathing and blood circulation are approaching normal. A respirator enriched with oxygen assists her. However, conscious skills are absent. At this point, until the swelling reduces, we are uncertain as to the extent of the head trauma. Her EEG is too discriminate at this time. There is brain hemorrhaging. We've administered steroids to reduce swelling. We're doing as much as we can to bring relief, but this will take time. She's under constant supervision. We'll conduct scans as conditions warrant. We need more information." His tone implied he couldn't add anymore at this time.

Alexis' words that morning before leaving for school eluded Samantha as she entered the ICU. Martin trailed his wife, eyes focused on his associated *little girl.* Sheer anxiety surrounding the incident paralyzed them. Staff finished inserting another IV while monitoring strategically placed electrodes. Machines whirled, recording and relaying data without interference. Seated next to the bed among a shower of wires and tubes, a mother clutched her daughter's hand hoping to squeeze *life* into her. She felt Alexis' cool, faint pulse. Her daughter's brokenness overwhelmed Sam to tears.

During the ensuing week, Martin and Samantha shuttled to and from St. Luke's. Christmas Eve arrived without festivity or decorations, no tree, no gifts, no guests. Each day's lack of improvement in Alexis' condition compounded the probable severity of her injuries eroding the chance she would survive. Occasionally, she stirred, but with no conscious activity. For Sam and Martin, hope for her recovery resisted the anguish and thoughts of losing her.

The inevitable death of her father and the possible loss of her daughter threatened Samantha's life. Dr. Pearson and Philip helped minimize complications. Philip maintained Gus' therapy schedule. Cautiously optimistic, Dr. Pearson always spoke affirmatively, but never committed to the certainty of Alexis' recovery.

Fluffy white crystals descended from above to a silent landing, adding to the existing foot of snow. Martin sat motionless in the rocking chair, enchanted with nature's serenity. Outstretched branches weighted with snow raised the heavens. They temporarily lifted his agony, provoking him, igniting a flicker of fascination. Throughout the frozen earth, plant and animal life endured with only nature's protection. Two hours passed and daylight surrendered to dusk. No traffic passed. No positive news came.

Gus rolled to his side, shattering the young father's hypnotic state. Gus stared intently at his nemesis. Morphine, Gus' habitual partner, relieved his pain and transformed his temperament. Fatigue forced him to a supine position. His spirit fought the consuming spread of pancreatic cancer. Martin thought Gus was aware of Alexis' hospitalization, but often his responses seemed to indicate otherwise.

"It's time I went to see my granddaughter." His voice was faint, yet clear and precise.

"We can't fight this snow," Martin countered.

"Hell, we been fightin'," he breathed heavily, "we been beatin' the shit out of each other for years. This snow ain't nothing." Pain surged in his abdomen and chest.

Martin assumed he succumbed to morphine, drifting back to sleep, but the lumberman persisted.

"I'm of no use here. Alex is waiting to see me."

Martin observed a physically and mentally exhausted man. "You're delirious, Gus."

"My ass, I am . . . Wrap me in my blankets and help me outside." He closed his eyes, summoning desire, gathering strength.

"I've antagonized you to no end . . . and I don't intend to stop now."

For the first time in days, an inspired smile captivated Martin. Gus' enthusiasm energized him.

"Get your butt outa the chair or I'm pumping up with so much juice I'll fly outa here." Gus winced as he coughed.

Martin approached and centered the feeble body on the blankets. "I don't understand."

"I think I can give you what I managed to take away for so many years . . ." His voice faded as he slipped into sleep.

The morphine induced nausea dropped Gus' weight below ninety pounds. Martin carefully bundled his longtime opponent in blankets and carried him to the truck.

Martin slid Gus onto the front seat. He cradled Gus' head on his lap. Like a content papoose sprawled across the bench, Gus slept.

Martin paused to resolve his dilemma. To stay home with Gus, might cost him precious time with Alexis. On the other hand, driving Gus through the storm as the man ordered might accelerate his demise in Sam's absence.

Acting decisively, Martin barreled the four-wheeler into three feet of powder. Instead of four miles, St. Luke's might as well have been four hours away. If stranded, Gus was guaranteed death in the cold or, without medication, death in some stranger's house on Christmas Eve.

Capitalizing on occasional clearings, he maneuvered within three blocks of St. Luke's before high-centering his truck and sliding off into a ditch. Snow packed beneath the weight of the frame lifting it off the ground.

Martin cut the engine. "Damn it!" He shattered the surrounding silence.

"What?" Gus cleared his throat on cue.

"We're stuck."

"So," Gus fired flatly, "you got two legs."

Martin grinned again resigning all reason. Reaching behind the seat, he pulled forth what appeared to be two tennis rackets and opened the door to lace on the snowshoes. Frigid air flooded the cab. Carefully, he lifted the terminally ill patient. Like carrying a sack of potatoes, Martin supported Gus' head above his body. One unfortunate jolt could possibly break his neck.

Flakes tickled his cheeks. "This is great," Gus sighed, "I love it out here. Let me loose to wander the sacred circle."

Thrilled to be outdoors fully immersed in nature, Gus erased all of Martin's reservations.

Automated street lights flickered. Snow encapsulated red, orange, yellow, green, and blue lights scattering a beautiful spectrum across the glowing white horizon unlike any Martin ever experienced. Heavy snow covered evergreens and pines accented the masterpiece. Profound quiet suspended life, inspiring eternal awe.

"Gus, you gotta see this." Bending to one knee, Martin propped Gus upon his thigh like a ventriloquist. He held the palm of his hand behind Gus' head to support it upright. Enormous flakes showered the wonderland.

Gleaming eyes wiped gloom from his unshaven face. Graced with a brief reprieve, he exclaimed, "Magnificent! Are we living on the edge, tonight, or what!"

No storm could deny Martin of his mission. He folded Gus' legs before him and arched Gus' back into his chest to carry his partner. Bobbing back and forth, Gus absorbed the amazing scenery. Martin often sunk to his knees, but he always kept Gus elevated above the snow. A surrealistic beacon in the night, "St. Luke's" illuminated the darkness.

Martin paused to rest after falling once again.

Gus labored to speak. "What'd you make that urn for . . . ? You made my job a living hell, and now you want to bury me?"

The old logger's tone challenged the activist. Uncertain Gus approved of the urn, Martin hesitated to respond. With his rival's back to him, Martin had no expression, no facials to interpret. Quiet, Martin assumed he failed Gus. He felt alone, as if his genuine efforts to nurture a relationship with his father-in-law had, in essence, driven him into isolation.

"I like it, Martin. It's special . . . well crafted.

Martin's heart rolled in his chest. Gus' acceptance affirmed him. Revitalized, Martin sprayed powder as he charged forward!

"Martin?" Gus gurgled.

"Yeah."

"You could have designed some fancy turquoise in-lay."

Martin embraced him with laughter.

While nurses arranged a bed adjacent to Alexis', Samantha scolded, I can't believe you brought him here during this storm. You could have killed him."

Standing in a puddle of melted snow, Martin shrugged like a defenseless child. "He told me to . . . and . . . I'm glad I did."

Fighting anger, her patience collapsed. "Are you crazy?"

Pausing thoughtfully, his eyes targeted hers. "Yes, tonight, I think I am." He embraced her fears, hope, anger, and courage.

Martin gently positioned Gus' head on a fresh pillow. Sam laid her head on her father's shoulder, something she longed to do on so many occasions. Her tears trickled along his neck. Lying on his side, Gus reached across to caress his granddaughter's hand.

The golden hue reflecting from the streets below filtered across the room. Hours passed. There was so much to share in the eve's stillness, what was, what is, and what could be. Martin gathered Samantha to his side. He massaged her fingers and watched intently.

Gradually, Alexis' eyes opened. She oriented herself to foreign machines and a web of cords and tubes. Mystified, her parents stared in wonder as if she were unknown. Alexis sluggishly rolled to her side and reached for grandfather. Gently touching his stubble face, she whispered, "I'm here, Grandpa. It's okay."

Tenderness softened his weary eyes. Gus mustered a smile hearing "Grandpa" resound from his granddaughter's lips. He rested a fisted hand over Alexis. Samantha embraced them both, weaving her fingers into her father's fist. He loosened his grip releasing the small twig his daughter had given him on her porch the day he'd arrived. "I'll be with you always. Merry Christmas!"

Merry Christmas © 1994
written by Tim Morrison

Dedicated to my Uncle Bud, a man who enthusiastically shared joy, enjoyed nature, and encouraged others to do the same.

Snow Runner

"No, not intentionally . . . sometimes, we're just out a control. We believe we have control, but we don't. And before despair strikes . . . your spirit takes over . . ."

Mannheim Steamroller's "Carol of the Bells" rattled my rear deck just before the national weather service issued their daunting forecast. Despite warnings, I defied the blowing snow and fired-up my '69 Chevelle. Those lacking respect for blizzards sweeping across the high plains often found themselves stranded or worse, frozen in a shallow grave. I recalled a time when I used cattle guards to bump steers free of snowdrifts created by forty mile an hour winds. I towed their frozen carcasses to rendering plants for puppy chow and protein shakes. Fish tailing right, my jacked up cherry red super sport rocked me back to reality. Southwest winds pounded us.

Angela, a Tri-Delt socialite I'd met only hours earlier, heard from a friend of a friend that I was driving home to Trenton, an economically depressed farming community in western Nebraska. Her parents spoiled her with a flashy Firebird, but Angela feared spending Christmas buried adjacent to some stray steer in a bar ditch. I assured her I was well equipped to maneuver through the worst winter storm. I began to regret I had not left a couple days earlier. However, I needed extra cash for gifts and decided to cover my debt working as a grease monkey for Roger, a diesel mechanic. College, auto parts, and Christmas left me bankrupt. I recycled Andrew Jackson's direct flight from employer, passed me to the merchant.

The towering unicameral capitol in Lincoln faded into the night as Angela and I followed a clear interstate 80 west. I knew no speed limit. Sleet taunted me as it shot across my hood. Determination overruled caution. I yearned to exchange stories with old friends, to eat mom's fried chicken, and harness my sisters, especially three-year-old Clarissa. Should I attempt to dispel Clarissa's innocent belief in St. Nick, mom threatened, she'd refuse to wash my laundry! I avoided Santa's workshops and tales of St. Nick. Consumers accelerated my saturation point when the jolly, plump red and white look-alike posed for holiday pics a week after Halloween. Of course, Angela defended the North Pole marketing attack. I didn't mention any of the gifts I stashed in my trunk, knowing her suggested preferences were impending. Her exclusive tastes conveniently nourished her partnership with her parents who owned Old World Imports in McCook.

Nervous anxiety permeated Angela with countless stories of Greek week and social functions. Some I selectively attended, most I avoided. Fraternal conformity didn't excite me. Sleet evolved to flakes. Ice sealed the side panels of cars occasionally passing in the opposite direction. Because visibility dropped dangerously low, I focused on the highway dividing line. I stopped twice to clear ice caked to the wiper blades. My eyes burned. In a white out, a fractional mistake could strand us both. In case of disaster, I continually registered the closest farmhouse to memory.

After three hours, a detour in Arapahoe directed us onto a county road. My experience on gravel forewarned me. Snow and ice had conquered it hours ago. I selected an alternate paved route. Although drifts would eventually bridge across these as well, paved roads were the last to collect blowing snow. However, this icy, heavy snow narrowed our window of travel.

Fueling stations in the sparsely populated west always closed early. My hot gas guzzling Chevelle ran extremely low on fuel. Driving on a thick transparent sheet, we passed through Hedley toward Cambridge. Depressed conditions devoured some communities leaving skeletal ghost towns. I raced through Wilsonville at 45 mph, station in sight.

Speeding beyond prudent visibility, I broke my concentration from the fluorescent road stripes. Suddenly though the white curtain, lights fastened to blockades spanning the highway flashed. Angela screamed a terrifying death knell as I slammed my brakes. We spun 180° sliding within inches of wrinkling red's chrome tail against the segmented orange, black, and white barriers.

Adrenaline flooded my heart tumbling erratically within my chest. Blowing snow reduced my world to a 25-foot radius. I clutched a flashlight from beneath my seat, stepped outside, and adjusted my bearings. Off to the shoulder, I noticed a construction entrance around the blockade. I estimated we were between a mile and two from Wilsonville. Too low on fuel to back track to the last opened station, I steered toward Cambridge, ahead not more than 10 miles.

Opposed to Angela's suggestion to go begging for fuel in Wilsonville, I proceeded. Petrified, fear suspended her. I eased off the pavement. Creeping forward, my Chevelle tilted slightly. At that instant, I firmly engaged the brakes to avoid another thrill ride into the unknown. White darts flew by as we slid sideways out of control. Preparing to roll, I squeezed the wheel with one hand and braced myself against the ceiling with the other. I heard myself boldly lie.

"Hold tight! We'll be alright!"

Jolting to a stop, terror forced her silence. If she hadn't been choking me, I would've assumed she was dead. Maneuvering out of our predicament was futile. Bailing out to evaluate the situation, I escaped her *better* idea!

We were stuck on ice wedged between the frozen bank of Bad Medicine Creek and the cab of a submerged pickup locked in the ice. Bridge out . . . and we're out!

I reasoned we'd climb the embankment to the pavement and follow it back into Wilsonville. Next, we'd have to impose on some one's generosity for the night. Big Red fell prey to the drifting snow. I slipped into my coveralls, handed emergency gear to Angela, and pinned a spare sleeping bag and blanket beneath my arm.

Whining, Angela sarcastically refused, "Are you terminally insane? I'm going to freeze to death."

"Either face freezing or suffocate alone."

Headlines flooded my memory of a trapped couple intoxicated with carbon monoxide exhaust. In our situation, the lack of fuel eliminated that possibility.

Angela's arduous climb to the plateau perturbed her more. Pausing I asked, "You smell smoke?"

"I hope your pile of parts bursts into flames."

I chuckled to myself. The concentration of fumes from her cologne was enough to sustain a blast! Imagining an explosive fireball was more dignified than ole red rusting in Bad Medicine waters.

Downed power lines whipping dangerously in the wind snapped brilliant sparks. The ice heightened Angela's fears wondering lost in the blowing snow, but she managed. Bounding through drifts, we nearly collided with errant steers wandering single file along the highway. With faint visibility, I was afraid we might have traipsed past our ghost town, when suddenly my flashlight penetrated the swirling snow, reflecting off dark windowpanes. Our eerie hike into deserted Wilsonville took longer than anticipated. We traced the boardwalk railing toward the local pub, Lodgepole Hole. Snow buried the panels of a pickup and a luxury automobile parked in front. Flickering lights through the windows guided us to the threshold.

Hesitantly opening the door, distorted shadows hovered over shelving scantly stocked with merchandise. A fire set our faces aglow, bathing us with heat. We were the apparent spectacle among strangers.

Leaning against the bar, a large man who obviously ate more than he sold issued a raucous, "You ain't no doctor."

Embarrassed, my face flushed realizing I failed his expectation. "I slid over an embankment next to a pickup frozen in the creek."

"Yeah, that's John Garvey's truck. He'll have to wait for the thaw . . . You ain't goin' nowheres, tonight. Just as well come on in and make yerself at home." His swollen cheeks squashed his eyes. His straggled beard reeked with chewing tobacco. As he stepped closer, his rank body odor gagged me. Crude, but congenial, he crushed my hand in his. "I'm Enos Holensby. Call me Enos, or just 'H.' I own this here place." His eyes traced Angela's silhouette from head to toe. "Not too often we get 'em as pertty as you are, in here."

Her vicious aqua eyes pierced his as she distanced herself from me. "She 'pears mad at you, boy." He spit into a pickle jar and hoisted his sagging pants to his enormous waist. Anywhere else in the country, Enos would be collecting unemployment. "What da ya think the weather's gonna do out there?"

What a stupid question, I thought. Without exception, during the summer, beneath pleasant skies, farmers ask the reflex question. "You think it's gonna rain, today, in the same breath as 'how ya doin'?"

Before I could enlighten him with our obstacle course through a forty-mile an hour blizzard, a frantic voice ordered, "Someone get more firewood."

Angela approached a man earnestly attending to someone lying on the floor. Abruptly, she ran into me crying. A man with abrasions covering his face commanded, "Bring more compresses and firewood!"

I isolated an injured woman in her mid-forties lying on the floor. Astonished, I stared momentarily at the fleshy fibers protruding from deep lacerations. Tiny sparkles speckled the floorboards beneath the woman's head. Removing logs stacked next to the fireplace, I cautiously positioned a few onto the glowing embers to refuel it. Blue, red, and yellow flares illuminated the room. Dancing shadows veiled the critical nature of her wounds.

I instinctively accepted the soaked crimson compress while Angela exchanged fresh cool ones. I watched his trained hands methodically adjust a splint on her forearm.

Enos' putrid breath fogged his assessment. "They came out of a two person plane crash . . . probably not far from where you stuck yer car. His wife don't look too good. He's not a much sight better." It explained the smoke I detected at the bridge. Enos played the suspicious detective. "Says he's Doc Nolan out of Chicago flyin' to Jackson Hole."

The doctor's supple fingers stitched tissue together using nylon thread unraveled from his coat. He fought panic as knowledge and lack of equipment ignited frustration. I felt grossly inadequate offering help.

"Find a plane out of this forsaken hellhole. Otherwise let me work."

Enos failed to recognize sarcasm. "We ain't goin' in this. We'll get lost." The doc's brutal glare stymied Enos' yakking.

Dr. Nolan wrapped his wife in blankets. Although most of the bleeding ceased, she remained unconscious, a coma he diagnosed.

Gas heat maintained a bearable room temperature. We accessed my emergency light and Enos' flashlight along with dust covered batteries. The Lodgepole Hole was a hybridized under stocked convenience store and over stocked liquor store. I pictured Enos distilling moonshine in contaminated kettles and filling recycled brown bottles. I doubt he knew the difference between methanol and ethanol. Drinking his brew might explain some of his mental deficiencies.

Throughout the trauma, a woman and a child sitting inconspicuously on the fringe escaped my observation.

"Their little foreign job's parked outside. Them imports aren't made to handle our storms. Somethin's wrong with the girl . . . think she's kinda slow."

The child appeared confused, but composed. I stepped closer. Taking a knee next to the child, I attempted to comfort her. "May I get you something?"

I introduced myself, but the nine year old simply gazed at me.

"Lorie's deaf . . ." The woman dressed in business navy and pinstripes reported defensively. Her stern sterile visage offered little tolerance. "She's not learned to read lips very well, especially strangers."

Tension paralyzed us. Fortunately, bursting through the entrance from out of the night, an Indian not much older than me stomped into the room on snowshoes escorted by a distinctive Siberian husky.

"Merry Christmas! This is my kind of storm . . . snow, wind, cold . . . and **guests**!"

I hardly consider myself a guest. Captive was more accurate.

He awkwardly clapped across the hardwood wearing oversized footwear. He proclaimed humbly, yet candidly, "I am Snow Runner, spirit guide of the Ogallala! My dog is Aurora."

"As a child, ten winters had not yet passed through my life. Natina, woman of our tribe, was in labor during the winter storm of '84.' I ran for help. I ran for food. I ran for wood. A healthy baby was born. I ran and ran and my spirit grew strong."

Rage seized the physician. "What the hell is going on?"

Aurora snarled briefly, and then pranced toward Lorie. Wagging her tail, the husky licked the child's face.

"Ahh," the peculiar youth acknowledged the child. Six pairs of eyes absorbed the exuberance of the spirit guide. In silence, he gracefully manipulated his fingers performing sign language before the child's gleaming eyes. She smiled and delicately signed to him. He nodded wildly. His fluent motion navigated the awkward moment.

Snow Runner addressed the stringent woman. "As a mother, I do not understand why you do not visually speak in her world." Removing his purple knitted cap, he shook his matted coal black hair. Slipping a ragged leather satchel off her shoulder, he carefully lowered it to the floor. Untying straps around his feet, he removed a pair of sawed of wooden tennis rackets. In thick-knee high moccasins, he stepped toward Aurora and untied the dog's caramel pack.

He pulled forth a rustic cloth doll stuffed with straw and trimmed with black hair, green eyes and ruby lips. The doll's uncanny likeness of the child stirred curiosity. He graciously extended it to Lorie. Smiling timidly, she cradled her gift and weaved a pleasant acknowledgement.

Next, he delivered a cellular phone and handbag to the physician. "Your spirit cried out in the wilderness. There were beneath your wife's pilot seat." He paused for a moment.

Enos interjected, "Old Mr. Jacob ain't gonna be too happy 'bout them litterin' his cornfield with their aeroplane."

Ignoring the fact that Snow Runner retrieved the cellular, Dr. Nolan accurately entered number after number. Irritated with no connection, he shattered the device against the wall, scattering fragments in the darkness. Death threatened his motionless wife.

"Let her rest. She's just sleeping," the Indian youth counseled. "Your medicine is weak. She needs to rest."

"What kind of ridiculous conclusion is that? Your spirit talk is garbage." Irritation surrendered to exhaustion as the helpless practitioner leaned back against the wall. Dried blood splattered his cashmere sweater. Fatigue weighed heavily as he gasped, "My wife is dying."

"Nobody knows the mind of the Great Spirit." Snow Runner asserted.

Unrolling his bedroll, he requested a hot toddy in a bowl for his companion. Enos poured a shot of Jack Daniels with honey into a bowl of water. Aurora quickly lapped the mix. She curled beside Lorie, still cuddling the doll at her side.

Plotting her assault, the female executive accused, "You're rudely impulsive."

"I speak what I know to be true. As a guide, I am obligated to present what you deliberately neglect."

"My spirit's doing just fine," she stated emphatically.

"I'm here, because you **believe** that." A discreet smile creased his lips.

"I send her to the best schools with outstanding instructors," the woman justified.

"Why? Do you not like your girl?" he innocently inquired.

"I work for the most prominent designers in the world. We create image, and ultimately, power, in the individual. I provide only the best."

"You know all about cosmetics and making money, but you do not share your daughter's experience. You know nothing of her world. You send a little girl away to learn how to speak in your world, one glamorized by false promises . . . you try to convince people they can buy what they are not. You equate appearance with depth, when in reality, they're mere illusions."

The Ogallala's mystique eclipsed his grubby appearance. Cleanliness was no priority. His coveralls were soiled and littered with patches. Yet, he derived unique insights with innocence. Enos had seen him once before. The guide was not a resident from around Wilsonville. Unsettled with events beyond coincidence, I resigned to observe.

I arranged some cushions against the wall to relax. Angela nestled in the sleeping bag next to me, more out of fear than comfort. Despite the anxiety **he** aroused, Snow Runner slept peacefully.

Dr. Nolan's activity introduced daybreak. Molded into the cushions, I searched the room for the guide and his dog. Lorie clung to her doll. Mom dozed in a contorted position parallel to her daughter.

Sprawled across the bar, Enos' snoring rippled the word work and distorted our dreams. Carefully, I rolled away from Angela and peered out the window. The relentless blizzard suspended dawn. Zipping my coat, I quietly snuck outside. Although I was restless, Snow Runner managed to vanish without waking me. No footprints traced his exit.

Enos abbreviated my investigation, hacking and spitting, staining the pure white blanket. A drift at the south end of the building aligned itself with the pitch of the roof.

"Thinkin' of leavin' us, are ya?" Curiosity begged my silence. "I wouldn't leave if I's you. Weird things happen when he's around."

"You referring to Snow Runner?" I sought clarification.

"Sure is. I know some Indians in the area . . . but he's bizarre."

Enos withdrew a plug. Flipping it into the snow, Enos pitched a fresh wad into his cheek. Drool rolled over his lip. He exhaled deeply. Discouraged, I resigned to spending Christmas Eve and possibly Christmas day in Lodgepole Hole. I'd miss Clarissa's ritual, arranging cookies, milk, and chocolates on the coffee table in anticipation of St. Nick's arrival. While sugar plums danced in her head, I'd savor a few snicker doodles and fill her tattered stocking with a stuffed koala. While reveling in tranquility, I'd mastermind St. Nick's travels around the world bringing gifts to all, even those in deserts!

Reentering, I forced the door against the intruding arctic winds. Dr. Nolan's repetitious formulas had not improved his wife's condition.

Torn between generosity or gouging us for money, Enos sluggishly offered us outdated pastries from his dingy shelves. I feasted on sugar-powdered donuts and hot chocolate while Angela professed roaches camped below. Staring at the worn floorboards, I recognized the brown stains punctuating Enos and his buddies' spitting sprees. A trail of maroon spots spiraled like glittering stars beneath Ms. Nolan's head. She had lost much blood.

Swirling and howling, arctic winds pierced the walls and floor gaps. It was difficult to determine whether additional snow was falling or blowing. Conversation was minimal and segmented, yet informative. Dr. Nolan was a distinguished internist at Northwestern. He confirmed his wife was a pilot. Her loss of control remained a mystery. He wasn't that excited about skiing, but she insisted they needed quality time together. His comments implied their relationship interfered with his extensive practice, creating divisive stress between them.

Divorced, but atop corporate ranks, Ms. Hansen dictated the cosmetic industry. Millions of dollars fostered her massive media blitz, "Image is Everything." Her models and styles adorned billboards and publications worldwide. Lorie's reality paled to her mother's hype. Attending an institute for the deaf in St. Louis, Lorie resided with her students and instructors. She became something to be modified to meet her mother's specifications.

Bestowed an appropriate title, Snow Runner stomped through the entrance, flushing dust into the firelight. Aurora bounded behind, darting immediately toward Lorie. She giggled as the husky warmed her playmate's face.

The brave's skin glistened with an evening bronze. Poised for a mission, he silently bore a heavier pack. Kneeling beside Ms. Nolan, Snow Runner sat back on his heels. He set the pack to his right. He handed Enos a clay basin and told him to 'pile it full of snow.' While he removed additional items, we naturally gravitated around him. Bewildered, Enos promptly returned with a mound of snow. The Ogallala leveled the basin in hot coals.

The wind subsided. Mesmerized, perhaps from the day's boredom, we watched Snow Runner methodically unwrap red flannel to reveal an intricately carved pipe, embellished with berry stains and quail feathers. Carefully handing the shaft with the cloth, he systematically packed ground tobacco into the bowl. From another pouch, he sprinkled small bundles of sweet grass into the flames saturating the air with a luscious aroma.

"You must draw the spice inside to become within the sacred space." The aroma engulfed us. Dr. Nolan remained acquiescent.

Snow Runner scooped a cinder from the coals and lit the pipe. He inhaled deeply, pulling air over the tobacco through the stem. He released a shallow cloud. Inhaling again, he closed his eyes and exhaled slowly. Serene, he proceeded to smoke. With extreme reverence, he generously offered me the privilege. I inhaled lightly on the pipe and choked on the smoke. He grinned, slapping me on the back. He demonstrated his technique. I inhaled again, much deeper. The bitter taste burned my lungs as I tried to exhale quickly.

He transferred the pipe to Angela. She passed it to Ms. Hansen, who, in turn, skipped Lorie and handed the pipe to Dr. Nolan. The circuit concluded with Enos. I expected Enos to manage the smoke's kick for as much chewing as he did. However, as with each individual, the effects were the same, coughing, teary eyes, and a choking sensation.

Once the brave possessed the pipe again, his eyes captivated Lorie's. He exhibited the proper techniques and exhaled. As he sat with his legs crossed before him, Lorie rose. He gently assisted her with the pipe. Closing her eyes, she inhaled and released a brief breath. Amazingly, she did not cough, but signed gleefully. He bowed graciously and tenderly embraced her cheeks with his palms. Taking the pipe, he set it in a cradle.

Paranoid, Enos whispered, "I told ya he was weird."

Dr. Nolan's patience expired. "This is weird. I don't know what kind of a wacko you are, but it appears to me everyone's sitting around getting high."

Snow Runner signed briefly to Lorie who immediately retrieved her mother's travel bag and surrendered it.

Ms. Hansen reached in protest, but he overturned her bag spilling an excessive assortment of pharmaceuticals and cosmetics in the center of our circle. Ms. Hansen stared embarrassed and angry. Dumbfounded, she appeared as I felt, reliving an incident when mom discovered me scanning photos in a *Playboy* conveniently hidden between the pages of *Life*. Ms. Hansen's insecure image crumbled among illusory drugs and disguises.

Snow Runner pronounced, "This is your medicine . . . temporary . . . and artificial . . . Industry owns you . . . The power you need is that of the inner spirit . . . I cannot give power, but I can guide. Only time and truth can revitalize."

He wrapped his hands in moist towels and reached into the flames to remove the large clay bowl. He placed it before Ms. Hansen. The mounded snow melted to steaming water. He poured amber oil into the water and submerged the flannel square.

He signed to Lorie. Reluctantly, she dipped her hands into the water. Wringing water from the cloth, steam slithered through the evening air. She diligently unfolded it. Dripping water across the floor, Lorie affectionately pressed the cloth to her mother's face.

Ms. Hansen resigned, releasing agony's moment. Lorie meticulously washed away her glossy lipstick, rouge, and dark eye shadow revealing a softer, more charitable face. Soaking the cloth, Lorie embraced her mother. I remembered comforting dad after I undermined his leadership when I publicly admonished his bill sponsoring unrestricted irrigation rights. I hoped hostility succumbed to compassion. Tears formed in her mother's eyes. Tears welled in my dad's eyes, also. I supposed they'd reasoned we clung to an ideal they failed to provide.

Snow Runner leaned forward brushing a tear from a stranger's cheek with his forefinger and touched it to his own. "From its cold harshness, snow cleanses and nourishes life. Your mask shields you from authentic beauty. You're vulnerability insures freedom. You appear natural, definitely stronger. Inner peace, truth, no one can take that from you."

Nervous, Enos cocked his head and spit into a pickle jar. He nudged me and whispered, "I told you. Weird stuff happens when he's around. He's lucky the lady don't hammer lock him and punch him out."

Swollen lacerations obscured the pilot's identity. Anticipating Enos' prediction, I resolved to intervene if Dr. Nolan's wrath emerged. His jaw and temples pulsed.

What I experienced in Snow Runner was far more than superficial.

Unraveling more sweet grass, he fed the flames. Enos added a few logs to the embers. The incense quickly quenched Enos' foul contribution to the aromatic ambiance.

Before the child, he massaged the air, creating sacred space. While Lorie positioned herself next to the injured pilot, Snow Runner unscrewed the bowl of the smoking pipe and with the cloth, squeezed a few drops of water over the tobacco to moisten it.

Fluent, artistic movements enthralled us as Snow Runner instructed Lorie. He handed her the pipe bowl.

His strategy became apparent to me. The spirit guide subdued the bitterness and the anger. *Who dared to pummel a deaf child?*

Within her silence, she pressed her finger into the bowl. Then, she gently smudged ash along the cruder sutures."

"You're contaminating the wounds." Dr. Nolan growled, forcing his hands away. Like a cornered coyote scrapping for life, his next fight would be his last.

"She's already contaminated," Snow Runner replied compassionately. "From ash, new life may spring."

Enos dribbled drool on his lap, missing the pickle jar.

"She's exhausted keeping your relationship together." Lorie applied ash over Ms. Nolan's eyelids, upon her cheeks, and beneath her lips, tracing her wounds.

Forthright, the Indian spoke. "Her energy was *so* low . . . and her spirit close to extinguished . . . she . . . probably *spilled* the plane herself."

"Intentionally?" Dr. Nolan argued, filled with rage. He lunged aggressively toward the guide.

Snow Runner leaned beyond reach. He wasn't finished.

"No, not intentionally . . . sometimes, we're out of control. We believe we have control, but we don't. And before despair strikes, . . . your spirit takes over . . . Entirely spent, your wife needs rest. Nothing you do is going to interfere now."

Pondering his actions as interference diffused Dr. Nolan's rage. He ignored the guide's presence. Attending to the fire, he retreated in silent reflection. Lorie returned beside her mother.

Grinning, Snow Runner delivered a gallon of filthy gasoline to Angela and me. "You need this."

I smiled and wondered if this was all there was. We needed much more. With my luck, he'd probably drained *this* gallon out of *my* tank.

Finally, cradling a slender object wound in blue flannel, the Ogallala exaggerated his presentation to Lorie. With apprehensive anticipation, she unwrapped an intricately carved pipe. Snow Runner's signs exuded joy. She mirrored his exuberance accepting it gracefully.

Saying nothing, he collected his gear. He rewrapped his pipe. He tossed a pouch of fresh home grown tobacco. "Thanks for your welcome, Enos."

Standing behind a man about to lose a woman he, at one time, loved more than life, Snow Runner touched the back of his palm against the physician's cheek. The doctor raised his right hand and clasped the guide's. The guide grasped it firmly. I secretly gave thanks for dear friends' encouragement during wearisome times.

Aurora pranced around a bit, and then nestled next to Lorie. Snow Runner spread his bedroll and quickly retired.

Desiring time to reflect, I bundled up and dissolved in night's stillness. A theater of a million stars showered me. The wind ceased. Through infinity, flickering stars cast violet hues upon enormous windswept waves of snow rippling the high plains. As if the first to explore a distant planet, I marveled at nature's spectacular snowfield. A jagged ocean frozen in time, the brilliant heavens illuminated the darkness. At that moment, it seemed to be no accident my car was concealed in snow. *I was a guest. I was invited* to witness this awesome creation. Eyes tearing in the frigid air, I rested. I paused in wonder, overwhelmed . . . a spectacle . . . a gift . . . the silence, the cold, the magnificence, the peace . . . all defied description. Tranquility and passion transformed ice and destruction.

I cherished my time in this sacred place, meandering back to Lodgepole. Each slept in his or her personal space. The flames enticed me to sleep.

Startled by loud, rhythmic thunder, all surged with the strike. Invigorating sunshine proclaimed Christmas morning even in Enos' filthy haven. A medical chopper landed, dispersing its crew. Ms. Nolan regained consciousness. Her condition remained critical. Paramedics acted efficiently. Little time transpired as a humble husband escorted his injured wife aboard the emergency airlift. We watched as if a raid confiscated two of our own.

Before Ms. Hansen and Lorie departed, Angela insisted on inspecting the drift beneath which my car was buried to supplement the stories she'd surely embellish with her sorority sisters.

Amongst the commotion, it suddenly occurred to me, Snow Runner and Aurora had disappeared once again, absent during the rescue.

Blinding rays reflected off the snow. Crystal blue skies bathed the earth in vivid color. Drifts cloaked deteriorating buildings. Corn stubble poked through troughs between six-foot peaks. Shallow waves spanned the highway. Thick ice sealed the pavement. Only the trail I'd cut the night before scarred the surface.

Tugging my coat, Angela beamed. "Isn't that your car on the highway?"

"I don't know how it could be." Elation quickened my pace.

When we reached the 'bridge out,' I surveyed the area. I saw the hollow out of which red had been entombed. In fact, snow still packed her underbelly. Circular footprints littered the snow surrounding the car and leading up the other side of the bridge.

Like children, we slid down the incline and stumbled across Bad Medicine Creek. We struggled taking two steps to climb one up the embankment to the other side. I hadn't locked the doors in case the keyholes froze in the ice. Inserting my key into the ignition, I fired red's sluggish 357. As she idled, my eyes traced the needle's arc across the fuel gauge to full.

In the distance, bright, contrasting colors captivated my attention. I opened my door and stood outside for a better view. Running along a cornrow between the crests of drifts, Aurora sprang at the heels of her companion. Both tumbled hurling a cloud of powder up into the air. I heard the spirit guide chuckle as he wrestled with his delightful friend. I laughed aloud as I watched them frolic in the snow. I had not idea where they were headed, but they were not headed my way. I figured our paths would only cross, but once.

I returned behind the wheel. Angela shivered impatiently awaiting heat as I eased into gear. Consumed in the excitement of going home, I will never forget Snow Runner had guided spirits.

A physician was healed, rekindling the love he'd almost let slip away.

An executive encountered a power, which no one could decimate.

A child realized her ordained gift as a visionary, a spirit guide.

And as for me . . . I told Clarissa I crossed the path of St. Nick on Christmas Eve!

Merry Christmas © 1997
written by Tim Morrison

Dedicated to Kathryn and Colleen, a daughter and mother who share the grace and love in their relationship and the world they experience through the communication of sign language.

Tomato Boy and the Junkyard Dog

Mysteriously, turmoil settled momentarily allowing me to recover from my exhaustive manhunt. Was it the invasion and vandalism of my fortress that upset me? Or was it that the peace I cherished one night when molten sparks danced before me teasing me with their enticing glow dissolved forever as a memory?

Hiding, secure behind towering concrete silos, I sat on an iron rail of the Santa Fe and sprayed my loot across the bedrock baking in the August sun. I tossed the large wrinkled envelop I received from my aunt as I accounted for a Snickers, beef jerky, peanut butter crackers, and leather gloves. Sizing the gloves, I admired them, clenching my fists, slamming them together.

From behind, I felt a strong hand wrench my neck. Another seized my arm. I struggled to identify my aggressor.

"You're not allowed around here. Whatta ya doing?"

In vain, I kicked a sandy hill of red ants scattering their chaotic fiery attack in every direction except that of my captor. In thought, I reconciled, "I'm only ten, and I'm too young to go to prison." My heart beat a rhythm of self-preservation. Desperate, I blurted without strategy, "I swear on the Bible. I don't know where this stuff came from."

A baritone voice reigned over me. "I've sworn on the Bible before. Drowned me in trouble. Could get yourself hurt around here." The Force released me instantly swiping the candy bar and crackers off the ground.

I faced him. His physical size and muscled frame smothered any possibility of immediate retreat. Running was no option. Fear raced through my veins. Periodically, I'd observed this man of epic proportion enter *We Chill 'em Saloon.* Saddled next to the bar, bombastic patrons hushed to a whisper. He never spoke to anyone, usually collected a pair of sixes and left. Rumor had it, he'd killed a man bare-fisted . . . beat him to death. *Holly Sugar* brought Picardo Tomas to town. They hired him as a construction welder on an enormous grain dryer, towering eighty feet. Now I faced extinction. Sweat rinsed his dark brown skin mirroring my own. Pink scars streaked his face like jet exhaust slicing a stormy sky. With a falcon's accuracy, his eyes threatened mine.

Well-defined muscles tensed his forearms. "The gloves, give them to me.

"No," I defied him, anxious to begin negotiations. "I'll give you something if you promise not to tell anyone."

Sweat dripped from his chin as his chuckle entertained. "What's in the envelope?"

Then I remembered. I considered briefly, making my break for freedom as my captor bent to retrieve the discarded envelope. I'd forgotten to remove the notebook my aunt mailed to me. Picardo pulled it from the envelope. He scanned a page. "Sit down."

Encouraged, I considered potential negotiations favorable. He folded the spiral cover and handed the book, page open, to me. He dictated, "Read this to me."

I grinned recalling my guardian's insistent warning . . . if I didn't learn to read, I'd end up working at *Holly Sugar* just like all the other 'wet-backs' in town. Picardo worked for *Holly Sugar.*

Intuition echoed, "Picardo can't read."

Picardo's command for me to read to him conceded the advantage to me.

"It's sunny in Chihuahua. I hate working in the field. The sun's burning me, today." I improvised proudly prompting him. "Want me to keep going?"

He extended a firm hand implying I should return the book. Confused, he stared at the page for a moment. He flipped the crackers and candy bar onto the bedrock. "I'll keep the notebook."

"Yes, yes!" I thought, suppressing the exuberance of sweet victory. I disguised truancy and the fact I didn't know how to read any better than he did. Starving, I dreamed of shade and devouring crackers and jerky. Secretly, I scoffed, "And he wanted scribbles in an old notebook. He can have them."

I began shoving my latest fortune into the postal envelope.

"That stays with the notebook," Picardo demanded firmly. I reluctantly surrendered it. Perhaps, I celebrated prematurely. The padded envelope provided the perfect cover slipping small items off shelves. I'd get another.

Migrants abhorred the label 'wetback.' Truth meant deportation if caught. I did not know if I was a wetback . . . surely, not. However, skeptical, I questioned embellished stories that our harvest crew swam the Rio Grande. I could piss a bigger river than what I remember of the Rio Grande cutting through the desert. In fact, migrants encountered greater risks of dehydration and missed connections while sneaking across the border during the dry season.

For seven months of the year, Golden Valley, a tiny isolated town on the eastern high plains stepping to the Colorado

Rockies, employs most of the alien population, migrant workers, as planters and harvesters. One either operates machinery digging up sugar beets and potatoes or one picks vegetables. Following the fall harvest, workers migrated to mother Mexico with their wages concealed. Many invested sweat equity to purchase a used pickup to sell in the homeland. In late March, with days of increasing sunshine, they'd return along specific routes usually beneath night's protection into the United States.

A short time before my father died a few years ago, when people referred to me as "no bigger than a grasshopper," I lived with my aunt and her four children in a two-bedroom duplex in Grand Mesa, Texas, a dusty wind-burned border town. That summer, cowboys drove longhorns down Main Street to the fairgrounds north of town. A parade of floats, short on extravagance and long on local advertising, escorted the Ranger marching band to kick off the Grand Mesa Fiesta. Rodeos, dancing, and fireworks thrilled fair guests for three consecutive nights. Although I preferred to live with my aunt, she couldn't afford to feed five mouths while at the same time serving meals in the local greasy spoon. My aunt found her brother, my father, lying facing down in the backyard dead. Word was my father died of a massive heart attack . . . too much smoking the weed. I never knew my mother. I heard she ran with some bandit to Puerto Vallarta. No one carries pictures to stimulate my memory. Being a mother didn't fit her job description, but being my parent didn't seem to fit anyone's lifestyle.

My Golden Valley, Colorado, relative bartered for my father's clothing and pickup. He also agreed to provide a bed for me. I'm a tomato picker. People assumed me to be average, but after I'd *acquired* my new gloves, I declared war on the horned yellow, black striped tomato worms. I'd flick 'em off the vine. Then I'd pop their bloated bodies squirting their iridescent green innards everywhere. Once, I started counting how many tomatoes filled a bushel, but when I reached one hundred, it exhausted me to think one bushel held so many. I picked three bushels an hour.

Early last spring, a twister cut a jag across the southern edge of town sideswiping the local grain elevator. Catastrophic winds pummeled a three thousand bushel grain dryer, twisting its eighty-foot frame and slamming it to the ground. It lay sprawled like a prizefighter over Santa Fe's tracks tracing parallel lines with the elevator silos. Creating adventure from imagination, children opportunistically converted the wreckage into forts for war games. I managed to shelter my stolen treasures through a maze in the fallen red galvanized giant. My crawl spaces between extensive narrow panels strangled claustrophobic pursuants.

"Yeah, I was pissed." I picked twenty-six bushels of tomatoes. Cabrones paid me for twenty-four.

The boss man teased me, "You imagined picking twenty-six bushels."

I reasoned, if I only got paid for twenty-four, then they should receive only twenty-four. The next day, while all the pickers including the supervisors were distracted eating lunch, I loaded a couple bushel containers in the back of a wagon and hauled them away. Perseverance prevailed.

Retaliating I pulled my fair compensation along the dirt road between the railroad and the grain elevator. Picardo ruled from a platform mounted high above the rail cars loaded with sugar beets long overdue for shipment and processing. He methodically clutched spoiled beets off the top and tossed them over the edge into a road ditch. I chuckled as I imagined Picardo browsing what probably appeared to be hieroglyphics as he thumbed through the notebook. Soon my nemesis heckled me. "Hey, Tomato Boy! You stole those tomatoes, didn't you?"

Glancing up into blinding sunlight, I barked, "These tomatoes belong to me!"

"And what'll you trade for my silence this time, little thief."

Annoyed, I declared kick-ass, take no-prisoners war. As my extortionist turned his back to me to inspect another rail car, I clutched a ripe tomato perfectly sized to fit my hand.

"Take this for your silence, wetback!"

Taking aim, I rifled the tight-skinned fruit precisely at his head. I splattered a direct hit upper-cutting his lower jaw. Ambushed, Picardo lost his balance and disappeared over the edge into an open cargo bay. Suddenly, my alarm of self-preservation reminded me. This man had murdered somebody. Had I fueled his intense desire to pulverize me? Towing two bushels of "fat boys" behind me dragged my escape to a waddle. I scrambled to my massive tangled refuge. Surrendering the tomatoes, I crawled, scraping my stomach on the warm metal maze. Slanted galvanized louvers used to release steam from drying grain locked permanently open over mesh metal sheets riveted underneath creating long horizontal channels of wide ducted work. Like looking through window blinds, I easily saw my invaders without them seeing me. Squeezing through a passage, I latched a sliding metal door behind me securing my defense chamber.

Shafts of light penetrated millions of mesh holes. Reduced to a mole, I wiggled on my stomach between familiar internal ducts and tunnels, closing additional hatches to prevent anyone from pursuing me. I peered between louvers to see Picardo standing once again atop a rail car. He cradled a large three-pound beet in his hand. Pitching with an underhanded rotation, he launched the projectile high into the air. Silence . . . where is it? Where is it? Boom! . . . Boom! . . . Boom! What vanished initially suddenly bombarded me. Incoming beets split upon louver knives. Rotting fruit smashed against the steel mesh peppering me with filth. Seconds later, additional foul-smelling missiles struck. Another hit at eye level, splattering waste and oozing through the mesh targeting my mouth. I spit hysterically lacking enough saliva to rinse my mouth of the slimy green shrapnel. Agents of decomposition, tiny white worms speckled my clothing feasting on fragments of decay.

"Hey, Tomato Boy! Do you surrender?"

I wasn't stupid. He was lucky he scattered his targets. Pinned like a coon I maintained my silence as not to disclose my position. The relentless air raid continued intermittently for the afternoon until the beet launcher grew bored with me or emptied his ammunition. I outlasted him. With caution, I snuck from my cubbyhole. I discovered the "closed" sign posted in the office window overlooking the truck scales. The workday expired. Picardo disappeared to his hideout.

"He wasn't so tough," I mocked, my glare clandestinely alert to my enemy's ghost among the hopper cars. Despite my pungent saturation of filth, I proudly wheeled my wagon of tomatoes behind me. Once again, I prevailed over my assailant to odorous victory.

Early December winds roared over the continental divide through Wolf Creek Pass forcing freezing air across the high plains. Often, I retreated to the grain dryer. Unfortunately, rats, raccoons, an occasional possum, invading my stash threatened our coexistence more than the rats in our rickety shack. Six, including my cousin, converged around a pine utility line spool conning one another. Arctic drafts exposed dense clouds of smoke rising from Mexican cigars and *Marlboros* diffused through walls from one room to another. *Coors* cans littered the kitchen floor. One of the floorboards broken during an unsettled score opened to a crawl space below. Layers of cans, trash, and cigarette butts recorded *We Chill 'em's* weekly specials dating my cousin's historical gambling.

"Francesco!" my slobbering cousin shouted. "Take this." A greasy, calloused hand tucked a crumpled twenty into my pocket.

"You, Cabrone, better come back with two sixes and a pot of change."

Without a compressor, the refrigerator simply protected bar food from vermin trespassing our shack from the crawl space. A case of *Lone Star* chilled on the back porch. Odds favored me embezzling the money before my inebriated cousin realizing I did so. I cut down trashcan alley. Distracted, I kicked the sole of my boots against Mr. George's steel barrel. Sparks flew.

Every abrasion fueled my confidence. I'd worn holes in the soles of my boots. I delayed executing my strategy to swap a pair from *Johnson's Clothing.* With gray tape, I secured a proportionate shingle scrap. Taping the scrap over the hole, gravel side down, I guaranteed traction in the snow.

Trucks circled *We Chill 'em Saloon* owned by Golden Valley's peculiar mortician. Walls oscillated to Willie Nelson crooning from a jute box angled out of a corner. Weaving the latest gossip, locals anchored at the bar ignored my entrance. Picardo leaned on the bar with his back to me. Avoiding paralysis, fear forced me into a booth, engulfed in a sea of darkness. Smoke-filtered light grazed his hardened face. Although he'd welded all day, determination hardened his eyes. Unassuming, he carried a six-pack under his arm as he tucked his wallet in his hip pocket. A cold breeze slapped me as he exited.

I gouged the floor with the soles of my boots, trailing the convict into the night. Beneath a full moon, I maintained a discreet distance. He hiked three blocks to the *Holly Sugar* construction site. Unlocking a padlock, he opened the rear doors to a severely dilapidated semi-trailer. Balancing the beer on the trailer's edge, he yanked the cord to a gas generator. Adjusting the choke, he tamed it to a purr. Lights illuminated the length of the interior. Wheeling acetylene tanks against some brackets stacked on the ground, he ignited a cutting torch. Feeding the fiery blue cone oxygen, he pierced the cold iron. A brilliant shower of violet sparks blinded me.

I crouched behind a tire, close enough to peek into the trailer. Much appeared to be junk. Small spools of electrical wiring, fabricated galvanized metal, and sections of iron beams similar to the one he was cutting dominated his inventory.

A white flash exposed my cover. "Find something you like, Tomato Boy?"

Humiliated, I threatened, "I'll turn you in for stealing this stuff." I kicked the license plate scraping few sparks in his direction fizzling any display of aggression.

"The trailer's mine. The Holly boys hired me to cut this stuff down."

"You scared 'em, didn't you? What's it like murderin' a guy?"

He exhaled a deep guttural laugh, one consumed in humor. He attempted to speak, but laughed some more. Light from the trailer reflected contentment in the welder's eyes.

"I never murdered anyone. I beat a guy up real bad. Enraged, I broke his face. I'm generally good natured, composed . . . but when I get angry, I get real angry."

"That how you got all those scars?"

"Most of them. Fought a lot a as boy. Trouble would escalate. I'd lose control. I apologized to *Holly's* supervisor, the guy I beat up. He hired me out of prison. I won't be here long." He swallowed a swig of beer and balanced the bottle on the bumper. Torchlight reflected off the mirrored trailer doors.

I frowned, "Can't believe you did that."

Beat a guy up?"

"No, apologize." I looked away confused by my enemy.

"Want a taste?" He raised the bottle as if to toast.

I ripped off beer from my cousin occasionally, but found his beer to be bitter. "What you gonna do with this junk?" I referred to the loaded semi-trailer.

"It's surplus or scrap from the new dryer construction."

"You gonna sell it?"

"No, I got it for a job in Texas." He retrieved a cooled metal sheet cut earlier and slid it across the wooden trailer bed.

"Looks like you need to raid a few more construction sites." I referred to the excess space available.

He smiled, gulped another swig, and changed the subject. "How's school?"

Fortunately, shadows masked my intentional lie. "It's good. What's it to you?"

"Shoot me your top three."

"Recess is good. Soccer's fun, but it's not a school sport. Next, lunch . . ." Momentarily drawing a blank, I recovered, "Oh, yeah, dismissal is the best."

"Read any good books, lately?" I smirked, remembering how I deceived him. "Any good stuff in that notebook?" Salvage man didn't know how smart I really was.

He shrugged his shoulders, grinning wildly, "Haven't really seen anything."

Sliding the visor over his eyes, he squeezed the striker and ignited the torch. "You're welcome to watch, but stay away from the tanks and torch. Sparks'll burn clean through you."

I don't know how much time transpired or even if Picardo usually worked that late, but for the duration of my visit, I felt all was right in the world. Miniature comets mesmerized me beneath eternity's stars. They appeased my soul. Picardo selectively cut a variety of galvanized pieces while I spooled waste wire.

Eventually, I wandered home. As predicted, the card game extended into the morning hours. Hard liquor washed all memory of the requests they'd made and the money given to me. I slid my boots off and, tonight, gently paired them on the floor. Closing my eyes, I rested in my evening's tranquility.

During December evenings, Picardo filled his "trash trailer" to capacity. Frequently, I stopped to watch him work. I assisted stacking items he determined to be useful, many more materials than I considered useful. I secretly named him the "Junkyard Dog" after a professional wrestler I'd seen on television. Picardo collected junk and he's a fighter. I think he grew excited to see me. Occasionally, he'd have an extra sandwich and soda as if he expected me. He offered little in conversation. Privileged, I proudly guarded his reputation.

Two days before Christmas, winter dropped snow off the Rockies. The shingle's utility in the soles of my boots proved essential. Remnants, drunken castoffs, surrounded the poker table worshipping food money prostituting itself in the center. Cramping of hunger, I sought jerky I'd stashed in the old grain dryer. In biting Nordic winds, drifting snow devoured it. As I approached, I cursed with anger. Numerous galvanized panels had been cut from the sides of my sacred space. Electric motors once mounted to the base had been stripped away. Impressions in the snow surrounded my fortress. Where was Picardo? Ripping a rusted pipe embedded in frozen earth. I marched ahead to assault Junkyard Dog's trailer. Rounding the enormous concrete pillars much to my dismay the semi-trailer had vanished. I exhaustively searched the streets, stores, *We Chill 'em Saloon,* and *Holly Sugar,* but no one had witnessed Picardo's piracy.

Like a salmon swimming upstream, I bowed my head into the wind and fought ice and snow pelting my cheeks. Soon the cold numbed the pain. Feeling an absence of toes and fingers, I trudged to my cousin's shack. Pausing on the wooden mid step, I kicked it harder than a sledge chipping a corner free. The shingle fragment taped to the bottom of my boot ripped, slicing the bottom of my foot. Climbing the threshold plunged my anger into apathy.

"Que paso, little man?" one card player slobbered, spitting into a coffee can filled with tobacco juice.

I ignored him.

Stacks of quarters before each player forecast an evening of braggart tales. Like a recluse, I entered darkness. Streetlight streamed through tangled blinds casting an abstract shadow on the wall. I exhaled deeply. The cold night exposed and gently lifted my hot breath. Bursts of muffled laughter and accusations marked the game's progression, interrupting my own.

Wrapping in blankets, I stared helplessly watching a lone pine layered in lights weave to dodge battering winds. Heavy flakes whisked by like sapphire bullets. Deteriorating walls creaked as powerful winds howled warnings of impending collapse. Mysteriously, turmoil settled momentarily allowing me to recover from my exhaustive manhunt. Was it the invasion and vandalism of my fortress that upset me? Or was it that the peace I cherished one night when molten sparks danced before me teasing me with their enticing glow dissolved forever as a memory? Was it that I liked the fact Picardo knew where I was despite all of my sneaking around? No . . . I resented his piracy. Buffeting the wind, the solitary pine dodged blow after blow luring me to sleep.

Thunder shook the floor. Brilliant light set my room aglow. I scrambled from my bed into my boots. Avoiding the poker game, I heard one holler. "Bout time you made a beer run."

I slid into the eye of the storm. Suspended in fascination, the *Peterbilt* semi-tractor I recognized as Picardo's rumbled to a stop, his dented rundown trailer in tow. Snow blurred the approaching outline of a figure forming before me.

Poised in soiled coveralls, he patiently offered, yelling over the wind. "You want to go?"

"Where?"

"Texas. You need some time to gather your stuff?"

I glanced at the shack flooded with cigar smoke and littered with beer cans. I shrugged my shoulders. "Nope." I turned my back on the shack.

Picardo opened the passenger side door. I climbed up over the diesel saddle tank. As if spying a rattlesnake, I'd locked onto a new pair of leather boots neatly positioned on the floor. Apprehensive, I looked at Picardo. "Those kinda small for you."

He nodded. "They don't fit me."

I immediately completed my ascent into the cab, ripped off those patched with tape and discarded them in the snow. My feet snapped into the new boots. The Junkyard Dog revved the *Cummings* diesel, shifting into low. The tractor reared and shook, dislodging from the drifting snow. The dash cast a fireside glow across Picardo's face. Warmth massaged my frozen body. I hadn't experienced penetrating heat in days. Onto the open road, six-foot drifts threatened our progress along the straight narrow Highway 87. Throttling down, the tractor rattled as it rammed ahead, blasting the snow barriers.

I questioned the wires poking from the dash. "Where's the radio?"

Tonight, the Dog lived in another dimension. "Can't deny a storm like this. Enjoy it. We're livin' in the blizzard's eye. When Nature displays such magnificence, you don't interrupt her. She's like the finest of women. She hates distractions and if you are, she gets really nasty." His wild smile cleared drifts long before we approached. Not to be denied, Picardo, graced with a mission, cut through blinding snow. Possessed by a Spirit, I quietly absorbed every moment. Silence. Eventually, the Dog's fine woman kissed him with rays of morning sunshine splashed over the horizon. He'd driven beyond snow's reach. I crawled into the sleeper wearing my boots and dozed. When I returned to co-pilot, darkness had once again settled upon us. An occasional farmstead sprinkled light across the high plains, beacons of Christmas.

Shortly after the midnight hour Christmas morning, Picardo steered his cargo into Grand Mesa, Texas. Festival activities buzzed. Neon colored piñatas swung beneath cords spanning streetlights. Children dashed from one game to another. The Dog's horn blared calling townsfolk to attention.

I recognized Aunt Juanita running along storefronts chasing us. She jumped to the cap, opened my door, and embraced me in her arms. Elated, her inner child's voice inquired, "Did you bring everything?"

"Oh,no."Picardo'seyesglancedaway,savingembarrassment. "I've got a load of odds and ends. There's plenty to get you started."

She reached across tapping his cheek with a mother's touch. "God bless you, son." Exuberance cushioned her leap to the pavement. Picardo tossed her some keys. Juanita and friends gathered anticipating his cargo.

Puzzled, my eyes delivered the inquiries to Picardo as to how he knew to come to Grand Mesa.

"Remember the envelope you traded away the day we met? Aunt Juanita's address was written on it."

He handed a bundle of books to me. I noticed the notebook I once offered as a bribe anchoring the bottom of the short stack. With a clever grin he finally reconciled the kid's shallow summer charade. "Retaliation. You learn to read and no longer feel the need to fake the garbage you created about Leon. You'll discover the words of your father. He desired more for you than he knew how to give . . . and much of it starts with an education. Here is where we'll stay. And that "junk" you stacked in the trailer will be incorporated into the school this town intends to build. I don't know that your father would have ever enforced it, but you will go to school and do well."

The school . . . while others talked of this dream, Picardo built it out of rubble. I didn't realize when Picardo said, "Here we'll stay," that "here" literally meant sleeping on top of the trailer beneath a canopy of constellations. However, after a short time, we settled into a place of our own. Some called it a "shack." I called it "home." Sometimes we do things to make it right with us. Picardo worked from within. His actions were not for me to judge. The gifts I received . . . I did not earn. They emerged from mystery, the depth of whose loving purpose I cannot comprehend.

I'll never forget the mystery of that Christmas eleven years ago. He's my dad. Anyway, the fall term isn't complete until I finish this final paper. I guarantee I won't miss my flight home. As I enter the main gate, I'll listen . . . tuning in to that familiar voice calling "Tomato Boy." Memories of showering sparks will forever illuminate the Junkyard Dog, scars of battles lost and smiles of victory . . . and mine of peace and home.

Merry Christmas © 2001
written by Tim Morrison

On Tiny Wings

A distant memory, like radiation filling empty space, unseen, yet full of energy, forced its emergence into my subconscious.

Silently, I translated data flooding my monitor. Pressing over my shoulder, Dr. Jeffries' reflection shook his head, gleaning critical details from cryptic sequences of letters and numbers.

"Like the others, these have failed to process cholesterol." I watched characters jump across the blue screen unraveling code to a dead-end.

Dr. Jeffries invested twenty-five years of life attempting to secure a polygenetic solution to Niemann-Pick Disease. "Once you analyze the filipin stained cells under the UV, you'll find an accumulation of cholesterol, as well." Filipin stain adhered to cholesterol producing a blue tint beneath ultraviolet light. The stain results were still to come, but only a sloppy error would alter the inevitable disappointing conclusion. Our cells, designed through gene modification, failed to modify or replace the gene expressing Niemann-Pick Disease. The last of several first generation trials completed Dr. Jeffries' grant on the genetic disorder. My mentor wandered toward his isolated cubicle, walls cluttered with the latest in published research, his notes scribbled in their margins, tacked to the walls.

NP-C children are born with a deficiency of sphingomylinase, a vital enzyme required to metabolize cholesterol and other lipids within the cell. As a consequence, excessive amounts of cholesterol accumulate in the liver and spleen and excessive amounts of lipids accumulate in the brain. Fatal neurological disorders ensue.

As a graduate assistant employed through grant money, I worked through Dr. Jeffries' present project for nearly three years. Ironically, with these discouraging results, my employment would cease.

I pushed away from my desk and hollered, "I'm stepping out for a cup of hot chocolate. Want me to bring something up?"

"No, thanks." His eyes focused on a transcript lying on top of a clutter saturated with data.

The desert breeze splashed my face as I sat at the edge of the verandah allowing my mind to drift. A distant memory, like radiation filling empty space, unseen, yet full of energy, forced its emergence into my subconscious. I sipped my hot chocolate.

"You've entered another dimension relatively quickly," Neil startled me. Gathering my composure, I cleared my throat, stuttering, "You know . . ., you know anything about the migration of hummingbirds?"

Befuddled, he grinned, "Not much, but I know you won't find them tanning in Arizona during the winter. Why? You planning on tracking hummingbirds for the National Institute of Health?"

"I think now is a good time I take a break."

"Sounds like good advice." He blew steam off of his coffee. Something about the environs of the lab restrained his more personable side, but outside it flourished.

My eyes triggered Arizona State students rushing between buildings consumed with semester finals.

"Any suggestions where I go from here?"

"I won't deflate the truth, Carly, but I think we have a better than even chance of securing future financial support. Obviously, if review boards pigeon hole us as conducting research exclusively on Niemann-Picks, we're in trouble. You know as well as I, with only two or three thousand diagnosed cases worldwide, few corporate folks including the NIH will invest where little potential revenue will be generated."

"But . . . ?" My voice begged for a morsel of positive news.

"But if the target of our research appeals to more universal applications of genetic therapy, regardless of the disorder, then I think some of the big guns may be more interested in funding us."

I chuckled hiding my deficiency of anything positive to share with my family and friends on my results.

"You think I'm over optimistic." I rarely experienced a lack of confidence in Dr. Jeffries and his strategies.

"No . . . I was just pondering some reflections . . ."

"Reflections?"

"Yeah . . . from seven years ago." I nodded, "Not so surprising, considering . . ."

The geneticist focused his attention. "You planning on sharing them, or teasing me?"

"Considering the season, Rudolph, Santa, and stuff . . . It's odd how this moment's luring me to another so many years ago. It was the week before Christmas. I was seventeen. I was living with my parents in the same house they live in now, in Emporia, Kansas. We'd enjoyed an unseasonably warm fall. During a peculiarly still night in the backyard, I playfully wove between the trees. I paused to lie in the grass and relish the lights that Dad had so artistically spiraled around each of three pines. The grass, thick and lush, was just beginning to brown. Interrupting my imaginary journey through my mystical forest, Dad lay on the lawn next to me,"

"Dreaming to fill your list for Santa?" He grinned, unaware he'd startled me.

I shook my head suspended between reality and my imagination that anything was possible.

"Well, if you were to think of Santa's list, what would you list at the top?" I can still feel the strength of my dad's arms wrapping around me, anxiously pulling me, and tugging me into his world.

I remained silent. Soon, I felt the warmth of his whisper. "What is it you want?"

"I want to hold him in my arms." My father squeezed me ever so tightly, as if my plea was a mysterious force acting to separate us.

I restated emphatically increasing its strength.

"I want Tommy to come back. That's what I want for Christmas."

My eyes traced the Big Dipper to isolate the North Star.

"Of course there was no 'Tommy' under the tree that Christmas . . . or on any other Christmas."

"I think Dad felt cornered. He concocted some lame story. He pointed to the stars and told me they were the rays of light through which Tommy watched over each of us from the heavens."

I blushed, embarrassed I was sharing a very personal event with the man who evaluated my research. However, I readily confessed.

"I've never been a big fan of Christmas. Often thought I might try another faith. Maybe I'd fare better in the miracle world . . ."

"Anyway, I squirmed, determined to capture my dad's eyes. I told him straight on, 'Stars in heaven ain't good enough. Seeing is believing! And until then, Christmas is just another day.'"

Unaffected, Neil shrugged. "Hate to admit it, but that's the way I've always felt."

Phoenix's vast array of lights illuminated the desert sky. I rattled on with my recollections.

"We magnify some cells, record some data, do some statistical gyrations and think we know more than anybody else about Niemann-Pick's. But we don't. We don't experience it."

"You can't believe how fast it happens. Nine years younger than I, Tommy followed me everywhere. Sometimes I'd tire of his shadow to the point of antagonism. I'd have hell to pay for it with Mom or Dad. I'd get so irritated when he'd pop me with his fork at the dinner table. Mom wanted flesh out of my hide after she saw the crater I cut in Tommy's hair. I'd carved out a sucker he'd entangled in it. Or when I sent him outside to piss in the yard because I was primping for a big night out with my friends."

"He was a normal child through four years of life. But the next year, seizures began. Tommy had difficulty swallowing. Carrying him was like lugging a bag of potatoes. He regressed from an energetic, coordinated little boy to an infant with no muscle control, stoic eyes, and slurred speech."

"I loved it when he slept in my arms. The day's struggles crumbled. I always convinced myself he was just a little sick and would soon recover to chase me again."

"Tommy died shortly after the fourth of July, a week shy of his sixth birthday."

Dr. Jeffries and I sipped our drinks silently in a world apart from all others. The cool breeze seemed to lift an invisible cloak sheltering a memory of my little brother. I heard him clear his throat purposely breaking our bonded silence.

"Initially, you asked me about hummingbirds?"

"Yes," I had instinctively guarded the memory of that balmy, winter evening with my father. I had inadvertently led Neil away like a doe running decoy to protect her fawn from predators. "On that night with my father over seven years ago," I surrendered, "a hummingbird darted around the tree lights. He stopped often, though not long before each color: red, orange, blue. He didn't seem to favor one. He flew to the interior of a branch and would disappear briefly before appearing again. Dad and I watched, amazed with his presence, mesmerized by his delicate features. My disappointment in my dad's explanation of Tommy's starlit presence lifted. The tranquility I was feeling before Dad joined me on the lawn, returned."

I shook my head confused and turned, smiling at Neil. "I didn't see a hummingbird tonight, but the memory of the little sucker sure surfaced."

I failed to contact Dad at home. Shocked when mom told me Dad was pitching a new business concept for management software with the Jayne Financial Group, I hesitated to interrupt him. His concept was one of the finalists. For a small university professor, the software sale would make an impressive capstone for his career. Significant opportunities were not as prevalent as he aged.

The cell rang a couple times before I heard his familiar voice. "Carly?"

"You closing the big contract?" I attempted the same positive spin Dad notoriously wrapped around new challenges.

"No, no. Just finishing breakfast." He sounded comfortable. "I have another hour before my meeting this morning."

"Mom says you've been in Denver a couple days. Evidently, you're dazzling Jayne Financial with your new product?"

"At this point, I'd say they're lukewarm. I'll answer to some of their tech people this morning and meet with the strategists, the decision folks, later this week." He paused, momentarily, prepared to field another question as if practicing for his interview, but I didn't have another. "So . . . what's up with you?"

"It really doesn't matter right now. I figured I'd catch you at home. I'm traveling home a little early for a break." I veiled disappointment in my voice.

"I'm guessing the results from your research indicated more discouraging results?" Keenly aware, he tried to be empathetic without engaging me in too much depth over the phone.

"It was expected," I admitted. "Surprised, I'm flying out, tomorrow at noon. Mom's meeting me in K.C. I'll let you go. I hate to cut this short, but I have loose ends to tie up in the lab before I leave."

"I can't wait to see you, Carly, love you."

"Good luck, Dad."

I closed my phone, relieved we didn't visit any longer. Frustration mixed with profound sadness rooted much deeper than I anticipated.

The southwestern jet stream carried me into eastern Kansas. A week remained before Christmas. Dad was scheduled to arrive home a few days later. My older sister lived in Seattle, working and caring for her two children. I assisted Mom as she played Santa's eager elf wrapping and packing gifts for her grandchildren.

After sharing a pizza and some amusing anecdotes about the grandchildren, Mom and I strolled the neighborhood, evaluating the commercialism of some decorations and the seasonal ambiance of others. Once we finished our circuit, mom returned inside to address some letters while I wandered into our backyard. I reclined on the grass centered in Dad's Christmas tree triangle.

Dad's spectral chaos merged with nature. A helix frequently ruptured leaving dark pockets where no branches were present to support lights. Other areas generously illuminated firefly metropolises. Above Dad's limited access, each tree tapered up into darkness, an outline to be seen, but not to be touched. A chorus of crickets and the occasional deep bass of a tree frog harmonized. Green grass streaked my dormant carpet. Stars, like fine diamonds, sparkled on a robust heavenly cloak of majestic purple, while clouds splayed like fingers stretched beneath a late harvest moon. Occasionally, I'd hear a car swish along a distant highway.

I bathed, soaking in a peace far too rare, wishing as I sighed that it last forever. I drew deep breaths as if savoring a passionate aroma. Closing my eyes, I relaxed enough to sleep, but remained alert, all too aware of the spirit of the moment. My eyes searched for life.

Was Tommy drawing on some wall somewhere? Maybe he was unrolling a full roll of paper plugging the toilet bowl . . . or growing a beard of peach yogurt, his favorite. I stared above through the outstretched arms of oaks clinging to their remaining leaves as I embraced a remnant, a wrinkled drawing framed by my sweatshirt. Crayons portrayed a sketchy array of fireworks, igniting my imagination as I envisioned Tommy's final scribbles. I embraced the drawing as strongly as if it was Tommy himself.

"Welcome home." My father's voice realized my vision. Humbled, I stifled surging emotions.

I stared into the reds, blues, greens, and yellows. Dad's slightest approach, a fractional step forward, would trigger my flight from my soul. He refrained.

"I thought you were pitching in Denver for a few more days."

He spoke softly knowing he encroached, but aware I longed to see him. "More promising clientele here."

I diverted emotion with humor. "This may cost you the big deal."

He lifted his chin and grinned. "Um . . . I have much more to lose than the 'big deal.'"

Wit succumbed as I choked back tears.

"I'm not so sharp." I began to audible just above a whisper. "I pray . . . and work twice as hard . . . I struggle simply to make incremental progress."

"You're incredibly bright, Carly. You're tackling a tremendous problem."

"Not very well, that's a fact," I scoffed. "Three years later and we're no closer than we were."

"Sure you are, you eliminated a major distracter."

He sat beside me on the grass. He lifted my arm away from my chest and pulled my wrinkled, scribbled picture into full view. "Fireworks, right?"

This was the first my father had seen Tommy's final drawing. I cherished that moment with my little brother safe guarding it deep within me.

"I don't know how Tommy drew that picture. Exhausted, he lay in my arms as I sat on the couch. The lyrics from "Moon River" . . . 'wherever you're going, I'm going your way . . .' had just rolled off my lips. He fell deathly still listening. In silence, I massaged his forehead, fearing I might breakdown. Suddenly, he tugged on my shirt. Staring straight into my eyes, a huge smile curled his cheeks. He gently cupped my face in his little hands and whispered, 'Carly, I'm in your eyes.' He was *so intense*, as if he lived inside me. No matter how hard I fought, or focused, or sealed off the outside world, I could not prevent his life from being taken from me. I gave him power hug after power hug, attempting to convey my undying love for him, something I don't think he understood. He burst into laughter, transforming my tears of fear to those of thanksgiving for the moment. I fell quiet staring at him again. I think it scared Tommy a little. I whispered, 'And I'm in your eyes.' Tommy leaned into me, content to listen to another song."

Tears filled my father's eyes. He searched the loss in my own. "I'd lost one child. And for years, I have feared losing another. You are the 'big deal.' I will not lose you." His warm palm cradled my cheek. "When you were seventeen, I never anticipated such a sincere, genuine request from such a silly Santa question."

I quickly reminded him as tears welled forth. "When I said 'seeing is believing,' you don't know how much . . . how much I wanted there to be a Santa. I fully expected to see Tommy, Christmas morning!" Tears overtook me. ". . . I'm still waiting, Dad."

"I know . . . I know."

I longed for his unconditional response.

"You'd had so much promising research leading up to this point. I'd listen to your positive updates. *But your unspoken thoughts were screaming*. I thought you might interpret 'seeing is believing' as Tommy miraculously communicating in some way to you, the critical link you needed."

"I won't say that is not possible, but for the vast, vast majority of us who pray and 'work twice as hard,' we must always keep our eyes open so that *we don't miss the miraculous in the obvious."* He displayed Tommy's drawing. "With no fine motor skills, Tommy drew this. Unable to speak, barely able to maneuver a crayon, he drew a picture of something beautiful and wanted you to have it."

Dad wrapped me tightly in his arms. "I love you, Carly . . . A day does not pass before I profess it deeply in my heart and hope you feel it sometime during your day in something you hear, taste, something you feel, or see . . . and I believe Tommy does also."

I lay in the comfort of my father's arms wrapped in silence. I focused on a flittering form poised on a branch next to a red light. A hummingbird paused for a moment. As I watched the fragile creature dance in and out between the colored lights, peace settled on his tiny wings, on a night I wished would last forever!

Merry Christmas © 2005
written by Tim Morrison

Dedicated to Joshua Noah Wilson, a little one we have lost . . . and to all of those who have lost little children. Know they are the finest of life's gifts.

The Intruder

Nobody knew we were here. We gazed in awe along the trail . . . the physical history of our journey buried beneath the purest snow.

In the beginning, there was darkness. Tears seared my frozen cheeks. Stunned, I sat on our concrete porch trapped in eyes reflecting death. And now . . . I've returned, suffocating in darkness I thought I had escaped months earlier. History's turbulence tossed my drifting mind back in time. Six months prior, a morphine drip saturated my body, relieving pain while fueling my few glowing embers of life.

I wrestled from sleep. Air Force Thunderbirds suspended in space, hanging from the ceiling, split the pictured Rockies. I stared at the ceiling anticipating them to vanish into the clouds. I reasoned . . . I must have ascended to a celestial waiting room identical to my bedroom. I anticipated human figures with wings to mystically appear and fly me to my heavenly destination. Mom promised that angelic aviators would escort her and dad to my new home among friends in heaven's mountains. However, as my weight shifted, I heard my bed's chronic creak ripple the hickory frame. Restrained to my right, I stretched to rotate my head. Fear raced from my heart the instant my nose grazed the swollen eyes and cheeks of my mother's embattled face. I retreated to my left. Anchored at my window, dad, weary and resigned of emotion, silently pleaded to a jury of stoic oaks.

Darkness buried me, alive.

"You cheated!" resonated in my ears, but neither parent defended me against my veiled accuser. Was I experiencing an out-of-body experience similar to the teen in the horror flick on cable?

Make-A-Wish dropped me from 4000 feet to train for angels. Soaring in a shimmering glider, we rode the rays of the sun painting the Arapaho Range. I broke the silence with a barely audible, "I did not cheat!"

To those in the professional medical world, my time at 603 N. Poplar had expired. All diagnostic predictions were errant. The Creator prepared no home for me, yet. Strength surged through my withering, fatigued 10-year-old body. My chapped lips fused together. Dry eyes burned. I tired of being tired. I attempted to lift myself in bed. I failed.

Mom awoke. Instinctively, her arms and her familiar sobbing wrapped around me.

I whispered. "I beat the cancer, mom."

Her squeeze made it difficult to breathe. Her tears massaged my neck. "It's the morphine, sweetheart."

Scared, I burrowed deeper into her arms. I defended, "I didn't cheat, mom."

While gazing among the stars, Dad surrendered trying to interpret 'why *his* son?'

"Dad, I'm not going."

He stroked my forehead. "I'm not going either. It's all right. I'm staying right here." The days' growth of his beard gently raked my cheek.

No one could hear the voice, my accuser. But erupting from my core, an intense voice drowned the other. "You are well." After four years, cancer quit fighting me.

We ran the gauntlet of doctors who probed, stuck, and cut me over the last four years. One referred specialist after another, each more perplexed than their predecessor, refused to proclaim me 'healed.' Shrugging his shoulders, Dr. Linblatz simply scribbled another appointment.

"I can't explain it . . . Life has a unique spirit of its own." Doc rattled each week we returned for additional scans and probing. Mom told Dad, Doc almost seemed disappointed I was recovering, fearing he might be challenged for malpractice.

Carly, a feisty mother of one, made the deciding call. "You beat it, Tom!" Grinning from ear to ear, she thrust her clinched clenched fist into the air.

"Doc won't say one way or another. How you so sure?" I wanted to break free from the cancer wing . . . to believe the recovering breast cancer patient. Carly clung to hope for me, like curled fingers clinging to a jagged edge over an infinitely deep crevasse.

"Your eyes, Tom. The fire's growing in 'em. They were pretty dim the last time I saw you. Soon they'll light up this room."

Perhaps eight years younger than mom, Carly leaned forward, wrapping a tawny arm around me. Closing in nose to nose, she pointed into her own aquamarine orbs. "See the fire in these, babe." She consecrated my forehead with the warmth of her palm. "We're gonna be alright, you and me." She laughed with the same thrilling laugh I had racing down Snow Mass Hill on an inner tube. I smiled thinking the rasp in her voice had softened since I'd seen her last.

I casually inquired. "How are the boobs?"

Choking on the audible, Mom flushed as if I'd asked about sex.

With an illustrative response, Carly cupped her chest. She winked, "You talking about these blossoms?"

"Yeah," escaped my lips before mom, suffocating, rapidly capped them with her firm palm. Endorsing the marvels of healing, Carly enticed the waiting room dozen.

"Wanna feel 'em?" Carly unbuttoned the top three buttons of her blouse.

"Carly," mom attempted to object, "I don't think . . ."

"Of course you don't. You're nicely endowed with a pair of the real things. I crawled through the muck, the pain, physically and psychologically. Everything's artificial, chemo, blasts of hormones. I want to feel attraction satisfaction, not the pity stares or the glances at what must have been. I'd gladly show these to everybody."

"Gotta admit, a morning in oncology never looked better!" An elderly art restoration specialist chuckled. He leveraged his cane as he dropped back into a seat a few chairs down across the aisle.

"Oh hush, Alan. Isn't nothing new for you!" Carly's smile graced Alan's presence. "A month ago, this ornery codger brought me a female Brazilian mahogany nut cracker! Imagine where the nut gets cracked?"

Alan blushed reminding her. "It cracked you up a notch or two!"

She discretely opened her blouse. "Here, Tom." Taking my hand, she traced their form.

I nodded affirming her. "Definitely have more than two teaspoons in there now! They feel kinda pointy like smooth spongy balls, you know, like my Nerf football."

"Tom!" Disgust fueled Mom's disapproval.

"Okay." I shrugged squeezing one breast. "Not exactly Nerf balls. Carly, it's not as warm as your ribs." Her sparkling eyes punctuated her smile. She'd cast no shadow, today.

"That is enough, Thomas!" Mom yanked my hand away from Carly's chest. Alan glanced toward admittance, avoiding capture in my mother's wrath. "Carly," mom began diplomatically, "I don't think this is . . ."

Once again, Carly interrupted mom's insurgence, spearheading her offense as she weaved a button between her fingers.

"It's a most appropriate action. I'd already died. I didn't think I'd see my daughter dance, ecstatic she finished kindergarten. When I lost my breasts, I forgot they weren't what made me really attractive. I balked at reconstruction. One day, your son asked me if I was a boy or a girl. I took his hand and fanned it over my buzz cut, flaunting the first haircut I'd had in eight months. You could bounce a dime off my chest higher than off the sheet of a marine's bed. I had just received my first two injections of expanders. Immense pain felt like I received two gallons, when in reality, it was a teaspoon in each. Anesthetics, pain killers, loss, nausea . . . all together I felt like dying at that moment . . . and then . . . Tom asked if he could feel 'them.'

"He told me about the special trip you made to the mountains to take him hang gliding and to ride horses in the back country without tubes sticking out of him. He was exhausted . . . micro assassins pulsing through his body.

"When he touched me, there was fire in his hands.

"I'm here because he touched me."

Carly hugged me tightly as if she was pulling me into her permanently. Mom stared, isolated and speechless. I sort of understood Mom's feelings because Carly didn't really make a lot of sense to me, except that I was part of her happiness.

When doctors initially observed spots on the bone of my hip, my parents and I commuted across the arid high plains from Limon into Denver. In Limon, Dad, self-employed, operated a rehab business while Mom cared for me. When my assault on cancer began, I reduced school attendance to two days a week. Friends drew pictures and played games with me. But once I began spewing food in reverse and wearing diapers for lack of control, I felt like a ratchety lion in a cage, one to be watched, but not one to play. Frequently, Mom gathered materials from school and assisted me with lessons and homework. Neighbors dropped off food, but kids quit coming to play.

After my initial surgery failed and extensive chemo treatments were scheduled, my parents packed and moved to Denver. We unloaded our U-Haul into a small house duplicated and sandwiched between two others located near a state park on Denver's western fringe. Dad said money in Denver didn't buy as much as in Limon. Dad wore his tool belt for a commercial construction firm to pay for therapy, which nauseated me. I didn't understand why having insurance was so important. Tempers occasionally interrupted my sleep. I figured the house owned my parents. I suspected Dad's insurance was not as strong as his sacrifice in surrendering ownership to his business. We needed Mom's income. As a librarian, Mom shelved books during the evening shift in the Broomfield County system. Mom played spelling games with me during the day and stamped readers' favorites at night.

The finest oncologists at Children's Hospital became my guardians. Doctors, nurses, clowns, and magicians offered hope my condition was a prolonged thunderstorm soon to pass. Most importantly, my mom or dad joined me though rarely together. I'd tire walking to the nurses' station at the end of my floor. Nausea preventing medicine drove me to sleep. Infections invaded weakening my system against future invasions. Many days, I'd sleep beneath the protection of Air Force Thunderbirds tacked to my ceiling while Mom or Dad's voice read "Little House on the Prairie." During my last eight months at home, words leaked.

'Reducing pain' and making me 'comfortable' replaced 'wiping out' cancer. But I didn't go to heaven.

Mystified, specialists, unconvinced, refused to boldly proclaim me 'cured,' despite encouraging diagnostics indicating I knocked out cancer. From apprehensive optimism to belief through exhaustion, my parents finally decided to restrict doctor visits to once a quarter. Rotations of injections, infections, blurred vision, and boring days relegated to a bed and additional surgeries graduated to the unfamiliar. After a two year absence from school, I was assigned to a home room, Colorado history, learning to read, and solving word problems.

Presently, I attend fifth grade and completed fourth grade reading and math. I'm not stupid. I overheard the school counselor call me a 'loner' because I don't have many friends. I hate school. Again, I'm the lion in a cage, but in a different zoo. I'm known as the bald kid with the metal hip. Although my hair's grown curled, team captains don't pick titanium-hipped kids for soccer or relays. I wouldn't choose me either. I waddle more than I run. I catch far more mosquito bites than I catch balls.

At the kitchen table, Dad assists in decreasing my deficit. He 'multiplies and divides' piles of screws before fatigue overwhelm his patience with a desire to drill me with one. School's similar to a clipper ship. During the day, I sit anchored in a dingy. The ship sails far ahead with the breeze. At night to close the gap, I frantically paddle to overcome the waves in its wake. Cancer brought mom, dad, and me closer together while, in school, the gap between survival and learning swelled with no end in sight. I walked like a freak among the living, no friends, poor grades, and no fun activities.

Today, I wouldn't be on my porch crying if Mrs. Henderson hadn't insisted that I go outside to play kick ball. Intentionally ignoring me, captains isolated me like I carried the pox. Coach Johnson waved me toward boys shoving to be first in line. "Tom, you're in with the team kicking first."

Because turtles move faster, I mastered imitating fence posts. While Coach Johnson organized the team on the field, I drifted toward the gym entrance. No one spoke to me. No one pointed to me. No one missed me. Slipping into the gym, I quickly hobbled the length of the hardwoods, exited under the red light and submerged myself in December's depths. Frigid air flushed demons from my soul. Inflated Santas and Snowmen cheered my escape. Drunk on freedom, I celebrated with a twisted jog.

Jousting with a broken branch at the gathering clouds, I taunted the weather gods to shower us with snow. I shouted, "Bring it on! What are teachers going to do if they catch me . . . kick me off the team?"

Initially, I chuckled, before reality slapped me sharper than the northern wind. There was *no reason* to hide. Why consider myself AWOL when nobody's searching?

Anger pumped a steam trail from my breath. Home was mine alone. I marched along our driveway crushing the dry remnants of autumn beneath my boots.

Ears perked high, slobbering saliva, and glistening ebony eyes, Kota raced toward me circling me with enthusiasm. Springing to my chest, my faithful Australian Blue Healer lathered my cheeks. Anticipating the customary headlock with a vigorous tummy rub, he continued pawing, licking my face. High-pitched whelps begged for affections that Kota lavished his upon me.

"Not now, Kota." I fired a jab at his nose which he easily dodged teasing me for more. He inherited a bluish black patch over his right eye like a pirate sworn to mischief. His front paws grazed my shoulders, lifting his head high enough to wink, coaxing me to take another shot. I popped my elbow with an errant swing. "Stay down, Kota! I don't want to play, now!" I commanded. No matter how bad my day might be, Kota lived exclusively to run, jump, and play with me.

Nearing the garage, I picked up a Frisbee lying on the lawn. Without looking, I muscled it, in frustration, as strongly as I could, flicking it high into the air. Like a missile, Kota fired. Leaves swirled in a vortex of his wake.

I turned to watch Kota's attack. Relatively, time collapsed. I saw a plastic saucer travel farther than I'd ever thrown one. Kota maneuvered in a world of unquestioned obedience. Blazing loyalty launched, defying gravity, ten feet in flight on an amazing diagonal. Muscular, athletic, artistic, Kota extended his jaw. The jewel in the bandit's patch cut the streak of a comet in flight. The Frisbee appeared to hover just beyond his reach. Refusing to be denied, Kota's determination snatched the trophy. And . . . then, dimensions from two different worlds collided while I watched from a third. The instant Kota drove his teeth deep into the soft plastic; the windshield of a car stole Kota's life, crushing the lungs of the soaring Healer! Two sharp, high-pitched yelps shattered the equilibrium, plunging my world into profound darkness. Barely braking, the coward discarded his victim like trash on the edge of the pavement.

Cradling Kota's broken body in my lap, I wept choking, pleading for his spirit of 'being' to return. His still, warm body cradled my disgrace and denial. A loyal friend I deeply loved, I have lost.

Tragedy hardened a scab over daybreak. Silence, weighted and cold, hung with heavy clouds triggered to burst as they scraped the tree line. Mom and Dad had yet to question Kota's absence. It was not unusual for Kota to disappear into Redbud's fringes hunting squirrels or chasing rambling coons. Reverently, I retrieved my backpack hidden beneath a plywood sheet leaning against the wall in the garage. I hoisted my sacred pack over my shoulders. Glancing back to home, I traced my daily trek toward Hamilton Elementary until the sight line to my house severed. From there, I journeyed into Redbud State Park.

Barren branches formed grand arches as I hiked along Kota's favorite trail escorting him for the last time. Oak centurions stabbed the heavens. Willowy snowflakes pounded dry leaves cracking the forest floor. I paused entranced with a vision of Kota lunging into a pile of leaves stirring chaos. Further into nature's mystic cathedral, Kota's bark echoed as he danced around a racing four-foot king snake. Thick, moist, cold air refreshed my mourning soul. I climbed the trail, loose with stones, guarded with timber to a bluff opening to a peaceful, sleeping valley. Drawing a deep breath, I lowered my pack and ever so gently, settled it against an enormous fallen sycamore, a reflective retreat where I'd rested often and shared many crisp, morning sunrises and radiant sunsets with Kota.

As if removing a rattle from beneath a sleeping toddler, I removed a compact military shovel from my pack. I trampled through dense vegetation to the left of the vast panorama. Although dormant, I recognized it as tangled vines of poison ivy. No one would disturb or venture near Kota's final resting place. Under normal circumstances, breaking the frozen soil layered with rock plates would have invited aggravation. The physical exertion forced my tears back. Satisfaction grew knowing I delayed the inevitable moment Kota and I would separate. I tossed the shovel aside. Grief ripped the ivy guard. What was once my backpack was now a benign lump beneath a three-inch blanket of snow.

Standing with my toes against the highest point on the bluff, I shared time with the Almighty. Showering snow buried the vast grasslands in tranquility. Like a Spirit immune to death, the gentle river, eighty feet below, wandered through the valley etching its signature into the limestone walls. A seamless necklace of ice-covered stones decorated an ornate shoreline. Life, invisible, thrived in the frigid water.

"Don't jump!"

Completely ambushed, I spun around and glared at Danny. "You crazy! Why would I do that?"

"Cause you lost your best friend and you think you don't have any friends." His triggered response left me gasping for air. Everyone knew Danny, a classmate, to whom I'd never spoken. Who wouldn't pick a guy who hit a home run every time he swung a bat?

"So what . . . I wasn't going to jump." Ironically, I remembered everyone encouraging me to run off the cliff with the hang glider when I had cancer.

"A neighbor said she saw your dog get hit by a car yesterday."

As if a servant to me, Danny glanced down and away, ashamed he broached my privacy. "I watched you dig for a long time. Many times, I thought I should leave . . . and . . . and . . ." He surrendered his hands and shrugged, "and I stayed."

Battling tears so that the intruder couldn't return to brag to his friends 'Tom bawled like a baby,' I frowned, "Well, you got to see. Now, get outa here."

Danny removed a glove and stuck it in his pocket. Unzipping his coat, he reached inside and pulled forth a small soft blanket. "I thought you might be able to use this." He stepped toward me, handing it to me. A tear trickled down his reddened cheeks. "I bought that blanket with my own money for my dog, Jack, when he died a few months, ago. While I was at school, my dad threw him in a dumpster. I searched a lot of dumpsters, even hiked to my dad's work to search their dumpster, but I never did find Jack."

Embarrassed, I clutched the cloth in my tightening fist. "I killed my dog." I returned Danny's blanket. Ignoring him, I uncovered my pack beneath the snow.

I gently laid Kota's head on my shoulder. I longed to feel Kota's affections, his warm tongue lathering my cheek. I cradled him as I paused, leaning on the sycamore. Kota slept like he'd done so many times nestled on the bed beside me.

Danny testified confidently. "The neighbor said it was an accident, Tom." Tears pooled on Kota's neck. I couldn't fight them anymore. They blinded me. "Kota was my best friend," I stuttered softly.

Danny uncurled the blanket I had wrapped around Kota and carpeted the bottom of the hole I had dug. He respectfully stood aside. I carefully arranged Kota onto the blanket. Not a single hair touched the soil. I glanced over my shoulder to see Danny squeezing his blanket in clinched clenched palms.

Humbled, I struggled to speak. "If you'd still like for me to have it, I'd like your blanket." Tears graced his innocent smile as he handed it to me. I graced Kota with it. Danny knelt alongside the dirt pile opposite of me. Our eyes met pondering one another.

I promised. "Kota's spirit runs here . . . and he will find Jack and they will run together."

Creating a place of dignity, together, in the absence of time, we refilled the hole with dirt and camouflaged it.

Danny sat beside me on the sycamore. Nobody knew we were here. We gazed in awe along down the trail . . . the physical history of our journey buried beneath the purest snow. A tunnel of stark branches and darkened leaves were transformed, glowing with brilliance. Light overtook the darkness . . . forever.

written by Tim Morrison

Home

He studied the smooth softness of her numbed left side. Creases recorded memories with each experience. Her intense awareness merged with another dimension of the wilderness hidden from him.

Outside the rest area, an unusually warm December breeze carried the musty scent of winter decay, flushing his lungs of septic gases. Responsibility for what he'd done lagged as he considered where he needed to go. His hope as if etched in a leaf fluttering from heaven fell with its descent. In no hurry to go to a place yet to be determined, he checked to see that bungee cords secured his athletic bag to the truck bed before sliding the key into the ignition.

Startling him, she appeared over the dash close enough to be a hood ornament. Her eyes stared expectantly. Her pleasant smile perched on hands folded over the wood carving of a black bear's head atop her walking stick.

He fired the V-6 and shifted in reverse buffering him from expectations. She shrank to a miniature in the rearview mirror as he drove to exit. She watched the brake lights transition to beacons coming back toward her.

He rolled down his window. "Mam, do I need to call for help?"

"Only if you think you can't handle a 66-year-old lady." Her smile swept to the sky on her right, while it sagged to the earth on the left.

"I need a ride to Gatlinburg if you're going my way?" She proudly held her Appalachian staff with her right hand. A withered left hand curled slightly as she fetched her hat clinging to her back by a cord around her neck. "National Park Service" banded the hat.

"I s'pose I can go through Gatlinburg." His tone indicated Gatlinburg was not his destination.

Caught staring, he noticed her left side to be compromised as she methodically planted her left foot stepping off the curb.

"I suffered a stroke six weeks ago. My left hand and foot have some catching up to do."

He reached across the cab and popped the door.

"Mind if I store my staff inside. My first supe carved this bear special for me. I don't want weather or man to mess with it."

He settled the head on an emergency blanket behind the driver side.

Her hands had worn a blond band into the dark stain logging the mileage she'd hiked over generations.

She leaned against the seat leveraging her left with force from her right leg lifting her onto the cushion. Sliding her leg over, she managed to squeeze inside to pull the door closed.

"Where you headed?" She figured she'd interrupted his plans.

"Nowhere."

She cocked her head compensating left and glanced at a boy too young to enlist for the military. "I can see you have a problem."

"Why's that?"

"Lots of places going 'nowhere' . . . easy to get lost."

"I'm Toni Huskey, park ranger with the Smoky's." She extended her curled fingers in a gesture of gratitude. "I been called boar whore, pine queen, otter cop. Not really names I appreciate."

The youth easily merged with traffic. He preferred solitude to sort through mental notes.

"I don't own a car and I'd get in trouble driving the Park's Jeep up here. " She chuckled, "I'm not as sharp as I used to be, to be getting into trouble. God knows I sure can't out run it."

He assumed the ranger had probably finagled a ride to Knoxville. Though curious as to the nature of her travel, he patiently awaited her disclosure.

"Came up to celebrate my brother-in-law's 78th birthday. One night, God up and called on my husband in his sleep after splittin' wood out in the snow all day. Fell asleep rockin' in his favorite glider watchin' the fire consume the wood of his labor." Her inflection offered honor. Imagining her husband's quiet determination, the boy's eyes scanned the pavement's yellow stripes

"I didn't think they hired old rangers?" He negotiated a lane around a refrigerated freight truck out of Alabama.

She confidently addressed his insinuation she was unfit. "I've been directing guests for the Park Service for thirty-nine years. Grandmother told me to get a job if I wanted to continue to live with her. The Park hired me to clean, work the gift shop, get coffee for the supe . . . lots of stuff. Can't imagine you're too interested in cleaning human feces out of soap dispensers."

"Nope. But the shoulder's wide enough for tales like yours." He teased nodding beyond her window.

"Anyway," she resumed to freely share, "one fine sunny morning, I'd just turned 27. The superintendent catches me jawin' the fat with folks rather than mopping the public bathrooms."

"Later, he calls me into his office. I feared the superintendent. I expected to be fired. He sits me in one of those good mountain-home chairs and asks me how 'I liked my job with the Park.' I said 'cut to the chase 'cause I'd been cleanin' up other people's . . . '"

"'Huskey, I'm not firing you.' He laughed. He noticed I liked flapping my trap and people liked listening. He said that I ought to be leading nature hikes. Seemed I knew quite a bit about the wilderness. I lacked for education, but the supe tested me lots to make sure what I know is to be true."

He weaved South into the mountains on Highway 411 avoiding the tourist gauntlet of go-cart rinks and Hollywood knock-offs. Though she knew better, curiosity drove her to pry for personal information.

"You going to remain a stranger?"

"Call me, Lisard."

"How do you spell that?" She seemed puzzled.

"L-I-Z-A-R-D." He pounded the letters.

She appeared confused. "That spells 'lizard.'"

"I'm named after the Hungarian physicist, Lisard. He wrote the famous letter Einstein signed warning Roosevelt of the Nazi nuclear threat. Lisard felt so bad about the bomb and politics, he wrote a book about dolphins."

Confused as to why a physicist working on the bomb wrote a book about dolphins, she politely chuckled asking his pardon, "Knowing about your name is already more than I know about physics." Feeling she offended him, she silenced herself anticipating home among the sun's rays setting the peaks' silhouette ablaze.

Rounding a wide flat curve, Lisard slowed as he passed a huge green sign anchored in stone masonry, "Welcome to Smoky Mountain National Park."

Lisard glanced in the mirror as if he'd expected his elder to be a bit disoriented with daylight extinguished. "You must have missed a turn back there somewhere."

"No, keep driving straight away. I'm a couple miles up the road." She felt the trees, the hills embrace her.

"People live *inside* the National Park?" he questioned with doubt.

"I do. I live on my grandmother's ground. She hated this park. Some wealthy folks vacationed back west. When they returned, they wanted to establish the first national park in the east, because there was none. So big money started buying up the ground all over. Grandma was one of the last to sell, but her home is still here. I chose to live here until they plant me on a hillside. Then it all goes to the people of these United States."

"That doesn't seem very fair." His truck weaved through the valley.

"Grandma did not like the establishment of the park, but I love it . . . When people drive past that sign and enter the park—it's like a vacuum just sucks all the bad stuff away . . ." A glimmer of light kissed her eyes as the ranger anticipated the mountains ahead. "I love it."

Toni felt relief with the familiar sound of gravel cracking beneath the tires as they approached her simple country residence.

Referring to the dry streambed bordering to her home nestled in a cove of oaks and hickories, he broke the silence. "You ever get trapped in there?" He eased his truck over the smooth stones to prevent scraping the under carriage.

"Naw. If the creek's rising, I park the Jeep on this side." She rattled her knuckles against the window motioning direction. "To cross, I hike upstream, not far, to the foot bridge. Rain brings opportunity for tubing these streams. Could get a might dangerous with rising waters. A tire tube is not a place to be when the rapids get wicked."

The truck rolled to a stop. Giddy as a child, Toni opened the door and tilted the seat to retrieve her precious staff. Before she could turn around, her chauffer delivered her pack.

"May I pay you with a meal?" she graciously offered, balancing her palms over the black bear's head. "Nothing like a good fire, some mountain home chili, and some company."

"Now, why'd you go and do that?" He refrained from smiling feeling hunger's growl pressing to emerge. "I could be a thief."

She curled her right hand around the wooden shaft and swept an arc in the air burying the bear's head into the lad's chest. She spoke in a manner of fact. "You can't take a whole lot from nothing . . . and what I do have worth stealing, you don't appreciate."

She chose her footing as she climbed methodically leading with her right up the steps to her porch. Recalling the labor of her deceased husband, Lisard respectfully cradled dry, split oak to the entrance. She paused and pursed her lips. "Shh . . . listen."

The teen's eyes searched void of reality.

"It's the song of 'creatures **not** moving—stillness, stillness of the night.'"

Slow and steady, Toni traced the trickle upstream along the rock wall she visited daily during her decades of tenure with the park. Outlining the rocky ridge, the sun ignited the timbers, gradually engulfing them. Clarity, exceptional visibility marked this rare day, a gift. The 'smoke,' a permanent resident of these hills, transformed to artful frost in the crisp cold air. Melting in the sun, it nourished all life to resurrect later as the smoke. Sapphire blue skies opened the heavens to the extended praising arms of oaks, hickories, ash, furs, and elms. Heavy remnants of a plentiful summer and pleasant fall, dry leaves and nuts carpeted the forest floor to cushion each of their guardian's steps.

Despite the park's millions of visitors, few ventured this illusory trail, believing it to be private property. The distinguished notes of a hooded warbler serenaded her.

"Help! Help!" echoed along the creek bed.

With quick cautious steps, Toni directed her staff a short distance into the forest up to Eden Falls. The same trickle of water pooled at the base of the falls and continued to meander over centuries' worn stones. A putrid sour odor alerted her of a creature trademarked throughout history dating among the Cherokee people.

Toni had won a few battles at the falls. A few days before her stroke, she and a fellow ranger climbed the trail on a blazing afternoon to the falls to discover young children dangerously close to sliding over the deceptively slick moss-covered boulders. She ordered a shirtless man wearing cut-off blue jeans to remove the children from danger. Decorated with violent tattoos, he littered the atmosphere with offensive four-letter bombs. One too many crossed her threshold. She instantly pinned him across the throat with her staff, bear head buried in her left hand. Strangling the man, she demanded. "Kids, get down off the rocks before you hurt yourselves over the edge."

"Generally, she's a nice old lady." Her partner shot an arresting glare at the man insisting he cease his threat. "Ya got yourself a Code W, Toni." Toni eased off the staff releasing the wimp she'd pinned.

The boy's screaming alerted her to the present danger.

Ferocity pulsed through her frame. Lisard, trapped against a grotto of ferns waved his arms frantically to scare a young male black bear to retreat.

Years of experience triggered her reflexes. "Calm down, Lizard, calm down. You got yourself a Code W." She stood firm, elevating the staff's carved bear face. "He's low on energy and not looking to waste it fighting with you."

"Easy for you to say. He's not interested in your old bones." The youth launched a stone striking its shoulder. The bear reared momentarily with a flash of teeth and a grunt.

"You hear that." Panic seized the boy's eyes.

"That's no growl. The hair on his neck isn't even raised."

"You can't see that," he barked.

"Exactly, if I could *you'd be in trouble.*" Despite the ranger's presence, the bear displayed little interest. "**Lizard**!" She focused his attention. "I want you to shuffle slowly my direction."

"But I'll be closer to . . ."

"He'll move away from us to the other side." She cut him short. "We're giving him access to that dirty rock and an escape route out from between us." She instinctively waived the potential victim toward her with her staff.

He slid like a shadow over the small rock alcove. The juvenile male stepped away from the human figures toward the wall the boy just surrendered. Stumbling past the ranger's staff, he rambled away from paradise.

"That monster could have eaten me!" He accused over his shoulder. Without realizing it, he'd outpaced Toni some distance behind him. She maintained her casual pace.

"You haven't enough meat on your bones to interest him. He wasn't about to eat you," She felt sad knowing she was required to file a report later for human ignorance.

"Thought I'd take a nice morning hike." He wiped his fingers on the pockets of his blue jeans. "Not only was I attacked by a bear, I got shit all over my hands."

"Quit exaggerating and let me see your hands." She inspected the greenish brown color swirled into a dark brown paste. With her forefinger, she swiped a sample from his palm, smelled it, and then tasted it.

"Gross." He wrinkled his face, gagging nearly dislocating his jaw. "You just ate some . . ."

"Reece's peanut butter cup," she intercepted his presumption.

The ranger paused to monitor the bear licking a dark smear off the smooth stones. "Someone baited the area with candy to get a cheap souvenir picture. Bears frequent this area because it's cool in the summer and sheltered in the winter. Aunt Jemima wanders into campgrounds to feast on pancakes and bacon, only to be tranquilized and relocated. She's never really been a threat, but will eventually pick up her third strike. We got some guys out of Wyoming trying to determine how sedated bears shipped sixty miles away manage to find their way back to their original site a few weeks later. Lucky for you I'm always on call. My job never ends."

Feeling nature deceived him, Lisard questioned, "I thought bears hibernated in the winter."

"We've had a string of pretty mild winters. The bears slow down, sometimes wander into town, but manage just fine through the winter. This range is loaded with dens for protection."

"And what's with calling me 'Lizard?'"

"I searched my encyclopedia Britannica for 'Lisard.' You spell his name S-Z-I-L-A-R-D . . . pronounced 'Zilard.' I'm sure you're Wiki savvy with all the other youngsters. Look it up. Somebody didn't get it spelled right." She grinned curious as to the boy's response. "His short stories, 'Voice of the Dolphins' dealt with the ethics of atomic weapons."

As they merged onto the well-traveled trail, she paused to examine the leaves of an enormous rhododendron. A heavy sigh blossomed from her frown. "There is little to no green remaining." She spread a leaf, largely turned brown, in the palm of her curled left. "They do brown in the winter, but not nearly this much. We lack moisture. This plant probably didn't bloom this summer."

Lisard raised his arms before him trivializing her concern. "But look at all the rhododendrons. They're everywhere."

"Yes, rhododendrons are plentiful, but there was a time when chestnuts grew like weeds." She waved her staff like a wand about to perform magic along the winding creek. "The chestnuts generally lining streams vanished due to prolonged dry spells." She pointed to a triangular evergreen. "The balsam woolly adelgid, an insect introduced from Europe, has killed most of the wild Christmas trees, Fraser firs. I've witnessed all this damage since I wandered these woods at your age. The national park has 75% of the firs in the world. Hopefully, with the decline in trees, the insect population should decline."

While he easily audited the vast grey skeletal remains among the healthy green firs, she wandered ahead anticipating time at the wall. Mosses and fungi decorated the stones stacked in a perimeter decades before the War between the States. Cornerstones worn to nubs marked the ruins of a frontier home.

Toni tapped a large rounded stone glistening from wear over time lodged into the top of the wall. "I spent many mornings and early evenings, sitting here watching adult otters dunk their young teaching them to swim. Like a midsummer night's dream, millions of fireflies spark a mating dance in this enchanted forest."

"When I was little, I caught a jar full from the back yard and let 'em loose in my bedroom." Lisard laughed recalling childhood innocence. "Mom opened my window to let them escape only to allow mosquitoes to join my party."

"My momma had me when she was a kid . . . not ever married to my daddy . . . so grandma raised me." A fondness in her eyes glazed the century old wall. "This wall kept the garden and house plants free from critters. Each day, I stop by this wall to talk to my grandma."

"You lived in a house here?" He wrinkled his face in disgust.

"'Til I was fifteen and the Park Service made us move into the house that cradled your dreams last night." She shook her head into a tremble. "Oh, Grandma was madder than a wild boar defendin' her young 'uns."

"The Park didn't buy her house?"

"They bought a lot of houses, but Grandma was forced to sell. She hated the Park Service." Toni repositioned her hat. "I wish she could see what this great land has become." She tapped the gold shield pinned to her Service green. "I think if she saw me wearin' this badge, she'd be proud." Toni flushed embarrassed, but snuck a peek at the heavens. "You may not think she's up there. God knows what people think, today . . ., but I sure do hope she's a lookin' down on me."

Pleasant crystal blue skies and a late Indian summer sun warmed a December hike to Alum Cave. Tired, they ascended to an overhang cut into the stone cliffs by millennia of pounding winds and cycles of freezing contractions and thawing expansions cracking and chipping the natural shelter into the cliff. Toni drew an accomplished breath as she claimed her boulder overlooking the valley.

"I'd hike up this trail in the winter in search of the snow line. No snow low, then I'd climb the mountain to find the snow boundary, a mystical place." She thrust her staff as a gavel on stone in nature's courtroom. "The park is loaded with mystery."

"Thank your Creator for this day!" She recommended. "He don't make 'em no better than this." The vast valley stretched to the Atlantic Ocean. One could easily see five states in the distance. Generally hidden but exposed in the winter, water released from behind dams controlled by the TVA cut gorges trimming the peaks of their jagged edges.

Toni recited, "Man has created some lovely dwellings—some soul-stirring literature. He has done much to alleviate physical pain. But he has not . . . created a substitute for a sunset, a grove of pines, the music of the winds, the dank smell of the deep forest, or the shy beauty of a wildflower." A smile as comfortable and as inviting as any refreshing spring on an humid August afternoon, swept Toni's face with youthfulness. "I memorized that quote to impress the superintendent as he evaluated one of my nature hikes with guests up through the Pass on the North Carolina—Tennessee border. The words of Harvey Broome, a naturalist, are cast in a plaque dedicating Smoky Mountain National Park as a United Nations Natural Reserve. Ya need to get up there sometime."

With the eyes of a red-tail hawk, she reviewed a distant model, the eastern pioneer village. She glimpsed the boy tranquilized by the river cutting into time and the rock below.

"I imagine your folks are a wondering where you've run off to." She interrupted his moment of fascination.

"Mom sells general stuff to doctors' offices like latex gloves, syringes . . . anything disposable, she sells it. She's always strung out on stress. Says it's a 'cutthroat job.' Dad's pitching the next gimmick in cellular. He's a big exec rollin' in the dough shacking up in his office." The youth swiped a stone from the floor and arched a shot into a circle of rocks hitting the natural goal. "Funny thing, I left my phone behind."

"Of course, they know my numbers, my ACT, grades that suck . . ." He calculated with cynicism, "If I was some sellable, tradable commodity, I'd draw their interest, I'm *best* in a portrait on a shelf."

He lamented, "I spent too much time as a telemarketer on a lower floor of Telecom towers."

"Dad get ya that job?"

Lisard shook his head. "Naw. I took the 7-11 shift."

Toni played exhaustion. "I've hit the hay by then. Who ya callin' at 11 o'clock?"

"West Coast folks. Once, Dad took me out to the garden on top of the executive tower. We talked about him meeting mom on a rafting trip . . . his first speeding ticket. At times, we just sat overlooking the ocean of Knoxville lights . . . I worked long hours to earn my appointment with him."

She inferred gently. "You don't sound too excited about being around your folks?"

"They're not bad people." He scored another stone. "They talk to everybody else, but me. And when we do talk it's nasty. It's strange . . . the more they're on the phone the more they're out of touch."

"How's school?"

"Okay. I kinda like science, but my grades suck. Mom's always on me about my grades and dad doesn't care anymore. They never ask <u>what</u> I'm studying. They hate my friends, but don't know them. I get angry. I get sad. I'm at one of those times. I don't like them very much."

"And do you know why?"

"No, but aren't they supposed to help me with that?"

"Everything comes with a manual or license these days. Not parenting . . . still an adventure." Toni curled her fingers around her staff and tapped a boulder as if to split it for water. "We need to be getting back down. Daylight's a burnin'."

They wound through bushes of yellow archways to a virgin stream, every stone cloaked with green. The ranger ran her fingers delicately over the moss as if reading Braille. She smiled reminiscing, "Rich kids who had real carpet in their dollhouses, laughed when they saw the moss in mine." She winked with her strong eye. "My Siberian forest cat, Trouble, would stretch a furry paw inside the living room and swipe my carpet. He'd wrestle with it and we'd laugh and try to take it back from him."

Lisard leapt and clung to a vine swinging above the rapids. Toni held her breath suspending him in her mind momentarily before watching him drop to the other side. They sauntered on down the trail together, each purging their lungs with the aroma of wilderness. Distracted by cliffs overhead, Lisard tumbled forward entangled in densely woven vines around his ankles.

"Dog hobble's got ya!" Toni paused to watch him attempt to break the knotted vines. "Bears will entice hunting dogs into the vines. Almost impossible to escape, the hunter becomes the hunted."

His elder continued ahead, expecting the youth to soon pass her on the descent. But, he didn't get far before she noticed him reclining on a log shaped like an elongated lower case 'h.'

"What animal makes its home in here?" Lisard inquired of the living, yet hollowed out lower trunk.

She joined him on the thick tree. "Cherokee mapped this trail well over 150 years ogo. When they and the Chickasaw went out overnight hunting, they'd stop and strategically tie rope high up around the trunk of a young sapling. The brave would bend the tree over and fasten it to the ground. The upper, leafy portion of the tree would seek and grow to the sun. Over years, the tree grew thick and sideways at the base then up. The brave returned to hollow out the center of the hump. At night or under bad weather, they'd lay inside the hollowed capsule.

Lisard peered inside. "Too many webs with spiders in there. I'm not messing with it."

She chuckled, "You would if the weather was bad or government troops were forcing you off your land, pushing you west."

"Suppose I could hide from a bear." He joked.

"You might dodge a wild boar, but not a mother bear." She grinned as he regressed to a child of discovery. "A bear has a keen sense of smell. On the other hand, a growing boar population threatens the park, even our bears."

"A boar's got a good sense of smell also, but he doesn't have the capacity to rip a tree open like a bear searching for insects or pesky children." She tapped the trunk driving out a hollow bass tone.

"Listen . . ." She froze chasing her left eye with her more mobile right. Lisard's eyes darted from ridge to ridge in sync with his rising heartbeat. Danger eluded him.

Her forefinger graced her lips. "Shh . . . listen to the voice of the rapids."

He plunged his sigh into complete silence. He studied the smooth softness of her numbed left side. Creases recorded memories with each experience. Her intense awareness merged with another dimension of the wilderness hidden from him.

"The whisper of nature's wisdom will not lead you astray like false marketing bombarding you with every stroke of a web site or billboard you see. You don't have to be something you're not. Nature does not care. She's all around you and she accepts you." Toni reentered his world, his dimension. Warmth erased fatigue.

His host lifted the blackened iron pot nestled in the coals and set it on the masonry before the fireplace. She disappeared into the closet equipped as a kitchen. Ruby sparks slithered with streams of rising hot currents while embers shed heat from the baked stone. Her guest stoked the coals with seasoned oak eventually resting it on the bed. Soon, blue fingers tipped in yellow cradled the wooden wedge then burst into large golden flames setting the room aglow. Shadows like spirits danced to celebrate a meal shared between new friends. She ladled a bowl of chili for each of them. A box of Saltines awaited the grand taste.

"You haven't really said much about your grandmother other than the Government pissed her off about taking her land into the National Park." His inflection begged to hear more of Toni's relationship to her grandmother.

The hostess settled onto a cushioned glider with her chili centered on a cutting board. She savored a bite. A mischievous grin lifted the evening light.

"Once Grandma took my cousins and me into the woods to show us the different kinds of berries and mushrooms we could and could not eat. We were like a litter of feral pigs runnin' around not payin' grandma much mind. Finally, without warnin' she told us we had to spend the night out on our own in the woods and fend for ourselves with what we'd learnt. We'd all gotten scared looking into the forest and seeing these strange eyes lookin' at us. We huddled close in a group until morning. When Grandma asked if we was scared we said 'no.' That made her madder than a momma bear for lying to her. She looked for a switchin' branch, but couldn't find one. She took off her belt and whacked us until our butts blistered."

Toni chuckled nearly choking on chili beans. "Those eyes we seen lookin' at us in the dark were Grandma's. She never left us by ourselves. Later, I figure she whipped us because we weren't learnin' what she's tryin' to teach us."

"Your grandma was a tough, gritty, switchin' old momma." He grimaced with his hostess nodding in agreement. "She knows a good mushroom from a bad one?"

"Pretty well, I think." Toni pointed her spoon to emphasize. "You see, Grandma made hooch, you know, moonshine with blackberries and mushrooms."

Inflating his lower lip Lisard wrinkled his nose. "That combo sounds awful."

"Grandma did some major taste testing!" Toni belched a deep guttural laugh. "At night, while looking for salamanders around the woodshed, I caught her singin' and dancin' in the back yard. It was ugly . . . watchin' her flop around back there in her big ol' heavy dress. She liked good hooch."

Toni clanked a flat note as she dropped her spoon into the bowl. "I wish Grandma could see me now . . . feel the peace and see the beauty of this park. I'd give her my badge." She slid her empty bowl with the cutting board onto the coffee table. Reclining, she permitted the fire to escort her to a dance with the warmth and mystery of the spirit.

Like an errant missile slicing the rapids, an otter frolicked in the glistening waters. Rays of sunlight pierced rising fog showering the ripples with sparkles. Toni approached the bank as a child sneaking up on her grandmother. She spoke softly in respect to the otter. "Good morning, Mr. Otter. Sadly, no snow for play this Christmas. You and the Misses have plans for the Eve?"

A strong whip of his tail launched him into a roll pausing belly side up on a flat stone. He basked momentarily in the sun smiling in response. "You see '*Lizard*' earlier?" She chuckled. "It was so early this morning, I heard him in my dreams. Thought he might be up hikin' the woods, but his truck is gone. Probably itchin' to get back on the road to 'nowhere.'"

Whisking her stick at the water's edge, she playfully flicked him with an ice-cold spray. Feeling a need to visit the wall, she maneuvered her staff in blind obedience to a place of reverence. Keenly aware of her environment, she recognized a stone out of place on the wall. She efficiently surveyed the area for humans, the only creature capable of placing the round stone.

Pinned beneath it, paper lay motionless like moss covering the supporting stone.

Dear Toni,

Thank you for being there. I'm going home now. You're a good ranger. Maybe you'll see my name cross your desk some day for a botanist's job. Tell your grandma 'hi.' I know she is proud of you. Take care of this special place.

Merry Christmas,
Jack Fisher

A broad smile swept Toni's face as she gazed through the sycamores into the heavens, "Keep a close eye, Grandma. Merry Christmas, Lisard."

Merry Christmas © 2010
written by Tim Morrison

Dedicated to the men and women of public service who generously give gifts of freedom, mystery, and insight to enrich the lives of others.

Notes

As stated in my introduction, it is my dream to establish a foundation to support charities through the Christmas stories that have been written. A future website is planned for additional access to all of the thirty four Christmas stories that have been written and the charities they will support. The following charities were designated for support through *Sharing Light.*

It's A World For Love	Humane Society St. Louis Foster Care Society
Great Christmas Artist	Smile Train
Return of the Spirit	Good Counsel Homes
Fourth Down and Tomorrow to Go	St. Jude's Children's Hospital
Spirit of the Ukraine	Amnesty International
Mystic Wind	Arc St. Louis Supporting people with Developmental Disabilities

Christmas Predicaments	The ALS Association
Snow Runner	Helen Keller International Central Institute for the Deaf St. Louis
Tomato Boy and the Junkyard Dog	Parkway South High
On Tiny Wings The	Belle Center: Non-profit serving children with disabilities Ara Parseghian Medical Research Foundation
The Intruder	Cardinal Glennon Children's Medical Center Siteman Cancer Center
Home	National Parks Conservation Association

For more information concerning these charities, one may visit their websites or for most the Better Business Bureau (BBB) Wise Giving Alliance. All of the charities above meet rigorous standards in supporting their stated mission.

Acknowledgements

So many people have shared wonderful experiences and support throughout my life. I am amazed when so much of what I have written reveals insights, enhancing my awareness to ask and to probe deeper questions. As mentioned in the introduction, I listen for the Whisper and write with a sense of revelation in the lives of others. I am grateful to the good Lord for His/Her patience and inspiration stirring the quiet of my soul. Often, I am not aware of where inspiration originates until further reflection. I'm also grateful for others who have humbly ventured into my life and touched me with wisdom.

I am extremely grateful to my good friend Barbara Moore for her endless encouragement and accurate editorial skills in polishing my final draft. Without her special talents, I'd have a number of mistakes left to the reader to tackle.

I thank Mike Howe and John Jauss for providing the ambiance each year for so many guests with Bunsen burners and "excited electrons" in flaming ions. I appreciate my students and colleagues who bring the excitement and anticipation of the season to me as they've awaited the revelation of the new Christmas story. To my family and friends thank you for the abundant encouragement in making this a tradition.

Thank you, Stephanie Zettl, a former student and presently a professional photographer who graced my first book with the author's photograph.

To mom and dad, thank you for the support in education and spirit for me to freely move into the world and to express my thoughts. They were the original source of my inspiration and gratitude. Thank you to Deborah Peters O.S.B. and Mary Faith Schuster O.S.B. for teaching me to write creatively with vision and to continue writing even through dry spells.

Finally, a special note of gratitude goes to my fondest critic, my wife, Terri. Though her recommendations were sometimes difficult to hear, she continued to be supportive and encouraging, giving me time and patience when I needed it.

Eva, my ten year old daughter, has allowed me to live the true meaning of Christmas. I have witnessed in her enthusiasm, joy, innocence, and anticipation the Light that is a gift to all of humanity. It is in the hearts of children where Christ speaks to us most.

To you the reader, thank you for inviting me into your thoughts and reflections. May the Light of Christmas touch you!